Playing Married in Summit County

Summit County Series Book 9

Katherine Karrol

D1715175

Cover Design by Ideal Book Covers

Background photo by Katherine Karrol

This book is dedicated to everyone who keeps their heart open to true love.

The Summit County Series

The Summit County Series is a group of standalone books that can be read individually, but those who read all of them in order will get a little extra something out of them as they see the characters and stories they've read about previously continue and will get glimpses of characters that may be featured in future books. The series is set in a small county in northern Michigan where everyone knows everyone else, so the same characters and places make cameos and sometimes show up in significant roles in multiple books.

This series is near and dear to the author's heart because her favorite place in the world looks an awful lot like Summit County. She is certain that the people who know her and/or live in the area that inspired Summit County will think characters and situations are based on them or their neighbors (or even on her), and she assures them that they are not. The characters and stories are merely figments of her overly active imagination. Well, except for Jesus. He's totally real.

Chapter 1

ZACK HUNTLEY TRIED TO stand still in front of the Christmas tree, but his nerves were winning the battle inside him. Time seemed to stop as he waited for his bride to appear.

He straightened his tie and adjusted the sleeve of his suit again. Mitch, his uncle and best man, snickered and nudged him. "Dude, I know you're excited, but stop squirming." Their seven-year age difference, coupled with the fact that they spent most of their growing years under the same roof, made the thirty-year-old Mitch more like Zack's big brother than his uncle.

"Shut it, Mitch."

At least his nervousness looked like excitement. He straightened his shoulders as he had done for barracks inspections a thousand times and took a deep breath, focusing on the scent of pine and cinnamon in the air instead of his own nerves.

Mitch whispered in his ear. "Don't you have something in between hyper five-year-old and recruit at attention?"

He shot a fake glare in Mitch's direction. "Leave me alone. I'm nervous."

Mitch met his not-quite-glare with another snicker. "That's what you get for planning a wedding in five days."

"Remember this in a few months when you're the groom."

He took another deep breath and tried to relax. If he had known how nerve-racking it would be to stand there waiting for Laci to walk down the stairs, he would have pushed for a courthouse wedding, or at least an even smaller ceremony in Mom's living room. As it was, they were in Evelyn Glover's elegant Victorian parlor. Evelyn was a close friend of the family and honorary grandmother to Zack, and her home easily accommodated the crowd of twenty.

The ceremony should have been at the church. They were going to need all the help God was willing to give them, and if getting married in His house would give them a leg up, Zack was all for it. Unfortunately, his frazzled bride insisted they do it anywhere *but* a church, and he had acquiesced, asking God to bless and help them anyway.

Before his thoughts could go down the path of the challenges that lay ahead, the bridal processional music started. His breath caught in his throat when Laci appeared at the top of the stairs on the arm of her older brother, Garrett. Standing there in the pale blue evening gown that matched her eyes, she looked even more like an angel than usual. She looked different with most of her blonde curls tucked into an elegant updo, but she was as beautiful as ever.

They had been best friends since first grade when their teacher sat them together, and they had been there for each other through every major life event. From the normal childhood milestones of losing baby teeth and getting driver's licenses to the more devastating losses of her mother and his leg, they were there, side by side. Their bond was impenetrable, and no distance, relationship, or life event could weaken it. They fit together.

Still, he was as surprised as everyone else in the room that he was standing there moments away from becoming her husband.

She looked as nervous as he was. Even from where Zack was standing, he could see the death grip she had on Garrett's arm as they gradually made their way down the grand staircase. Maybe the old stairs weren't the wisest way for her to make an entrance, but they had thrown the wedding together so quickly that there hadn't been much time for deliberating over details.

Between her bouquet and the alterations she had made to her dress, the baby bump she was so nervous about was invisible to the naked eye. The only thing those gathered could see was the beautiful woman walking down the stairs, about to become his wife.

When she finally looked at him and smiled shyly, he let go of the breath he hadn't realized he had trapped in his chest. The tension on her face let up a bit when he smiled at her, and he willed her to keep taking steps and make the rest of the walk to his side.

As they approached, Garrett gave Zack the nod meant to convey his approval of the union. He had given it a couple of days ago when Zack had asked for his blessing, and Zack hoped he would still approve if he knew the truth.

Once next to Zack, Laci transferred her death grip from Garrett's arm to his. No wonder Garrett was grimacing. The strength that made the two of them competitive in everything from driveway basketball and beach volleyball to cornhole over the years was now choking off the blood supply to his arm.

He tried to listen to Pastor Ray's words as they stood there, but the moment she reached his side, his thoughts had become consumed by one thing—the kiss. It was coming—the very public, very awkward kiss that they hadn't discussed when they planned the wedding.

The kiss that he had wished for since he learned about kissing was about to happen, and in front of spectators, no less. Sweat broke out on the back of his neck.

Chapter 2

LACI RYAN HELD ON to Zack's arm as if her life—or at the very least, her ability to stay upright—depended on it. She stretched up to whisper in his ear. "Are you sure about this?"

"Yes. Stop asking me that."

She tried to focus on Pastor Ray's words, but hearing about God's holy design for marriage sent a hot wave of shame through her. Shaking, she leaned into Zack and gripped his arm even harder.

He looked down at her and smiled, then reached over and loosened her fingers on his arm before covering them with his. "It's okay. I've got you."

As usual, she was comforted by his strength. She was so focused on using his arm to keep herself steady that he had to pull her hand from it when Pastor Ray asked them to turn toward each other to recite their vows. Handing her bouquet to Brianna Callahan, Garrett's girlfriend and her maid of honor, she took refuge in Zack's gentle brown eyes and the strong hands holding hers. They were doing this.

Suddenly she realized what was coming. The kiss! They hadn't talked about how they were going to handle that part. After years of wondering what it would be like to kiss him, she was about to find out. *Whatever you do, don't pass out.* She tried one of the breathing exercises he had taught her, but when she imagined his lips on hers, her lungs forgot how to work.

From the time she was a young girl, she had wanted to save her first kiss for her husband and had vowed to God that she would save it for her wedding. The irony that this would not be her first kiss, but it would be the first with her husband-to-be hit her like a hard slap to the face.

Chapter 3

THEIR GUESTS LAUGHED ALONG with Pastor Ray when he had to repeat the instruction to kiss the bride.

"I can honestly say I've never had to repeat that part before."

Zack and Laci laughed nervously along with them, then he reached out and pulled her into his embrace. Too embarrassed to look her in the eye, he kept his focus on her lips as he leaned down toward her.

When his lips brushed hers, they were as soft as he had always imagined they would be. He kept the kiss brief and chaste, but the brevity didn't stop him from feeling the zing down to his toes. Instead of feeling awkward, it felt like the most natural thing in the world, like their lips were specially designed for each other. It also knocked him completely off his bearings.

I just kissed Laci. Laci just kissed me. He was sure he was having an out-of-body experience right there in front of his closest friends and family. Not knowing what else to do, he held her tightly.

When Pastor Ray cleared his throat, Zack realized that they were still gripping each other. He was sure his cheeks matched the red in hers as they separated and the tiny audience clapped at the introduction of the new husband and wife. As he summoned up the courage to look her in the eye, he wondered if she had felt anything like the shock wave he had during the kiss.

Chapter 4

OH MY GOODNESS, THAT kiss! Zack's lips were just as strong and perfect as she had dreamed they would be over the years. For a brief and glorious moment, she forgot the circumstances of their nuptials and basked in the glow of being Zack's wife.

If only she had saved her first kiss for her wedding. Of course if she had, she wouldn't have reason to be marrying Zack today and wouldn't have just had the sweetest and most heavenly kiss she could ever imagine.

She couldn't look at him without blushing, so it was just as well that their friends and family were surrounding them and delivering hugs and congratulations, pulling their attention from each other.

Garrett lifted her off her feet and swung her around, then held her for a long moment. "Congratulations, Laci Lou. You've got a good man, and Mom would be proud."

She hoped he thought her tears were from sentimentality rather than shame, and she held on to him for an extra beat as she tried to get control of her emotions.

Mom. Maybe if she was still here, I wouldn't have gotten myself—and now Zack—into this mess.

Once her tears were under control, she let go of Garrett and accepted a hug from her new mother-in-law.

"Oh, Laci, I've prayed for this day for years. I can't imagine anyone I would rather have for a daughter-in-law and a wife for Zachary than you."

"Thank you, Cynthia. I'll do my best to be good to him." Even though her words were true, she hated that the wedding itself was a sham and that they were deceiving the people they loved most in the world. Cynthia had taken her under her wing after Mom died and had been the closest thing she'd had to a mother figure in the years since. Lying to her cut deep.

Zack interrupted their moment to steer Laci toward the library. "Pastor Ray has to go, so we need to sign the marriage certificate."

She gulped as she took his hand and let him lead her away. It was about to become official. Once out of earshot of their friends and family, she stopped him mid-stride to offer him one last chance of freedom. "You don't have to do this. We can just say we realized we were rushing things, and you can walk away."

"Laci, stop saying that." He led her to the stairs, and they sat together. "I told you when I suggested we get married that I was sure about this, and I've told you a hundred times since. We're doing this. It's the only way."

"I don't know how I'm ever going to repay you for this." A new set of tears started stinging her eyes as gratitude washed over her.

He reached out and pulled her into his comforting arms. "There is no repaying. We're doing this for the baby. That's that."

"I love you, Zack. You're the best friend anyone could ever ask for."

"No, you are." As they stood, he smiled at her and stuck out his tongue, making her giggle despite the tension she was feeling. "Let's go sign the paper so we can do what we set out to do."

Zack must have seen her look at the front door, because as they walked toward the library, he put his arm around her and pulled her close. "Don't even think about it, Bubbles."

Using the nickname he'd given her in first grade made her laugh and soothed her nerves. Even if the marriage was a sham, he was the perfect husband for her.

Chapter 5

PASTOR RAY GREETED THEM with a broad smile when they walked into the library arm in arm, laughing together.

"Congratulations, you two. I'm sorry to have to rush out, but I promised my wife I would be home in time for our New Year's Eve dinner."

"We understand, Pastor. We appreciate you doing this on a holiday, and especially on such short notice."

"Four days is pretty short notice. I usually don't marry people without having counseling sessions before the ceremony, but I felt a peace about you two from the moment you asked me." He handed the pen to Zack and pointed at the line that waited for his signature. "It's not often that I meet couples who have been best friends their whole lives, and I figure if you've been close this long, you know each other well enough to know what you're doing."

Zack focused on the paper so that he didn't have to meet the man's gaze. Even though they were lying for a good cause, it felt awful. *Lord, please forgive us for lying to a pastor. And please get us through this evening.*

When Zack handed the pen to Laci, her hand was shaking as much as his. Relief flooded him when the pastor put the final signature on the document after hers.

"I'm sure glad you two started coming to the church a few weeks ago. It was an honor to do this today."

Zack reached his hand out to shake the pastor's. "Thank you, sir."

"Can I pray for you before I leave?"

"Of course."

While he prayed for the marriage, Zack and Laci held hands so tightly that his fingers started going numb. He was sure she was feeling at least as guilty as he was when the pastor asked God to bless their marriage—especially when he prayed for any children that might come from their union.

When Pastor Ray walked out of the library, Zack closed the door behind him just in time for him to miss seeing Laci burst into tears. Zack pulled her into his arms again, an action which he had done more than ever over the past five days and one which he never minded.

Laci wasn't normally a crier, but between the hormones and the stress, she had cried every time he saw her lately. He was getting better at just letting her cry for a moment, and he stood there holding her while she got it out of her system. She got herself together so quickly that he was disappointed when she pulled away.

"I'm okay. I'm just emotional."

"I know." He wiped the last tear from her cheek. "I'm getting used to your tears by now. No worries."

"Thanks." Even when she was under a huge pile of stress, she had a smile that could both melt and inspire him.

"We successfully convinced everyone here that we had a whirlwind courtship and wanted to get married fast so you could do it in front of a Christmas tree, and we have a signed marriage certificate to show the adoption agency. We're pulling this off."

She nodded at him and took a deep breath. "For the baby."

"For the baby. You ready to go back out there?"

"I'm ready."

Chapter 6

WHEN THEY WALKED THROUGH the library door, Laci was ready to mingle with their guests and enjoy a nice dinner together, then duck out and go to the two-room suite they had reserved in Grand Rapids. She didn't expect their guests to be tapping on their glasses with spoons, rings, and anything else that was close by and staring at them, waiting for another kiss.

Zack had the same look of surprise on his face when she looked up at him. When he put his arms around her and leaned down to give her another peck on the lips, she closed her eyes. His second kiss was somehow even more sweet and amazing than the first one had been. Their lips lingered a beat longer than they had during the ceremony, and she was glad he was holding her up when she went weak in the knees.

There was a part of her that hoped that the guests would do that several times over the next couple of hours. Another part was sure that if they did, she wouldn't make it through the evening with her heart intact.

When they gathered around Evelyn's large dining table, Zack's mom was the first to stand and deliver a toast to the newlywed couple. Cynthia gripped the shoulder of her new fiancé, Wyatt Henry, as she began.

"Zachary and Laci . . . this is the day that I have spent years wishing for. This is the day, Laci, that your mom and I joked about when the two of you were in elementary school and wanted to do everything together. I'm so thankful that God directed Mrs. Coulter to sit the two quietest kids in the first-grade class together in hopes that they would help each other out of their shells."

She shifted her gaze to Zack. "Zachary, you told me the first day that you sat at the table with the shy blonde girl with all the curls that you were going to marry her. I promise I will listen better in the future when you make such declarations." She wiped a tear from her eye as the crowd laughed. "I couldn't be more proud of the man you are, and Laci, I couldn't be happier to have you as my daughter. I pray that you will have a long and happy life together."

Zack winced when Laci's nails dug into his hand. He leaned over and whispered into her ear as everyone else clinked their glasses in the toast. "Ease up a little. You're breaking the skin."

"Sorry!"

"It's okay." When he smiled and kissed her, she was glad she was sitting down.

Garrett was next, and Laci was afraid she might pass out. He grinned at her and walked over to stand behind her. "Laci, you have always been the best sister I could ever hope for. When Mom died, a cloud came over our house, but you were always the ray of sunshine that kept the family going. When you and I watched Dad take his last breath last summer, I knew it was going to be okay because we would get through it together." He reached out and squeezed her hand as she wiped her eyes with the other. "In those dark days when Dad was sick and after he died, there was one thing that brought a smile to your face, and that was a text or call from Zack. I kept wishing that you would see him as more than a buddy, and I thought you were crazy for keeping him in the friend zone."

He shifted his attention to their guests. "Fast forward to four days ago, two days after Christmas. Zack came to me and asked for my blessing to marry my baby sister. My first thought was, 'Finally!'" The crowd laughed along with Garrett, but his expression turned serious as he looked around the table. "My first words to Zack were the only question I thought was appropriate. I asked him what made him think he was worthy of my sweet sister. His answer? 'I'm not. I just want to give her a good life.' Those words were the key that unlocked my blessing for this union. Zack, you're the only man good enough for my baby sister. Welcome to the family."

Laci was a mess by the time Garrett kissed her on the cheek and shook Zack's hand. She tried to dab her eyes delicately, but when Zack leaned over to hug her, she hid in his broad chest.

As the dinner went on, she eventually relaxed. At times it felt like just another evening hanging out with Zack and their families. She could see that he was getting as tired as she was, and could tell by his slight limp that he was not only tired, but ready to get a break from his prosthetic leg. "Is your leg bothering you?"

"A little. It's been a busy week, so I'm tired. How about you? Are you okay?"

"I'm ready to drop."

"Okay, let's get out of here. It's a two-hour drive to Grand Rapids, and it's starting to snow."

Chapter 7

ZACK'S HAND SHOOK AS he put the key card into the lock of the hotel room. When the latch gave and he opened the door, he turned to Laci with a mischievous grin.

"Put your bag down."

"Why?" She narrowed her eyes. "What are you gonna do?"

He snickered at her. "You said you would obey me today in front of a bunch of witnesses. Put your bag down."

She giggled as she carefully set her bag on the suitcase he had brought in. "You know there's no one who knows us around here. We don't have to put on the wedding show."

"Don't care."

She squealed when he picked her up and carried her across the threshold. "Put me down! You're going to hurt yourself." She tried to wiggle out of his arms and stand up, but he wasn't budging.

"I'm a man, Laci. I'm a soldier and I've been in war. Carrying you is easier than the pack I had strapped to my back every day over there."

His declarations of bravado had always made her laugh, and she stopped fighting.

"Plus, my momma told me that a gentleman carries his bride across the threshold. If there was anything she tried hard to teach me, it was to be a gentleman." It was taking all of his gentlemanly training to not give her a real kiss right then and there.

"I'll be sure to tell her that she did a fine job. Now put me down before you break your back."

"You're not *that* pregnant." He didn't want to put her down. She felt good in his arms, and he wished someone was there to ding their glass and give her reason to offer her lips to him again.

When she giggled into his neck, he remembered that even though she was his wife on paper, she was really still only his friend. Grudgingly, he carried her over to the couch and carefully set her there before retrieving the suitcases and her tote bag from the hallway.

It was good to have reason to walk away from her for a moment. He was suddenly very aware that they were alone in a hotel suite, and he felt the heat rise in his face. It was a two-room suite with a living room in between, but it still felt weird. *Better get used to it. When you go back home in three days, you're moving into a two-bedroom apartment just like this.*

They had been alone plenty of times in their lives, but always as platonic friends, never as husband and wife who were pretending to be in love for the benefit of the people around them. And never as two people who had kissed a bunch of times earlier in the evening.

He pushed the thought from his head and peeked into the rooms. "Do you care which room you get?"

"Not at all." She sat on the couch, where she took her shoes off and started rubbing her feet.

After sizing the suite up, he put their suitcases into their respective rooms. "I put your stuff in the bigger room."

"Did your momma teach you that too?"

"No, I figured that one out all on my own."

She grinned at him in that way she had that had always made him feel like he could conquer the world. "You're going to make a great husband."

Chapter 8

IT FELT GOOD TO get out of her dress and stockings after watching a movie with Zack. Laci gazed at the dress and stroked the silky material after hanging it in the wardrobe.

It had been a good choice for a wedding dress. There was no way she would wear white under the circumstances, and blue seemed like a nice alternative. Since everything else about the wedding had been unconventional, no one batted an eye when she showed up in the elegant evening gown. She had sewn some pieces from a dress of her grandmother's into the bodice for something old, carried the hanky that Evelyn had given her for something new, and worn a necklace that Brianna loaned her for something borrowed to round out the old tradition.

When she opened her suitcase, she saw that Brianna had snuck a beautifully wrapped package into it. She opened the card, which said that since Laci hadn't had time to shop for proper honeymoon apparel, Brianna had looked for something special for her. The pale pink satin negligee with matching robe was stunning. The lace trim was delicate and feminine and was definitely honeymoon-worthy—for someone else.

So sweet. But this isn't going to be that kind of honeymoon.

She suddenly felt lightheaded and sat on the edge of the bed, careful not to touch the beautiful set. There hadn't been any discussion about a physical relationship between them once they got married, but she wondered if she was supposed to put the negligee on and go out to the living room. Between her dad with his overnight visitors after her mom died and Ronnie, the boyfriend she had broken up with before realizing she was pregnant, she had heard more than she ever needed to about men's needs. Zack hadn't said anything about it over the few days since they decided to get married, and he was the one who found the hotel with separate rooms, but he was still a man. She didn't know what to think.

She had spent most of the time since the differences between boys and girls had begun to show themselves trying not to think of him that way. As soon as she started noticing boys, she noticed that he made her feel different than all the rest. The other boys made her nervous, but Zack always put her at ease and made her laugh. He accepted her and listened to her, and since they'd been friends for so long, he was a part of her. Since he had never shown any interest in her in the boy-girl way, she had always told herself that she had to think of him no differently than she thought of her girlfriends.

Keeping him on that shelf in her mind after all those amazing kisses at the wedding was going to be a hard task. If she thought it was hard not to imagine kissing him—or other things—before, it would be nearly impossible after finding out just how wonderful it was to have his lips touch hers.

She put the beautiful set back into her suitcase under the rest of her clothes and put on her fuzzy pajamas. Even if it *was* one of those kinds of honeymoons, she would have felt too self-conscious to prance around in something like that. Any thoughts she might have had about being attractive, let alone sexy, were long gone. Ronnie had told her time and again that she was too fat for most guys and that she was lucky he gave her the time of day. Her body was no different at the end when he said that than when he showered her with compliments in the beginning, but he must have just lied in the early days to pump up her ego. By the end of the relationship, her self-image was as bruised by him as her body was.

Maybe it was good that Zack didn't look at her as a girl or think of her that way. He would only be disappointed.

Chapter 9

ZACK SETTLED INTO HIS bed and turned on the TV. He knew it was a bad habit to watch the news before trying to go to sleep, but since the day he had enlisted, he had been driven to know what conflicts were going on in the world. Being on partial disability due to Post-Traumatic Stress and the prosthetic leg propped against the bedside table, he knew in his head that he would never be called back to combat, but part of him always felt as if he needed to be ready.

He turned off the TV and tried to read, but then it started. Loud noises and flashes of light from outside the window tried to take him back to a place in his mind that he worked hard to stay out of.

Calling on all that he had learned at the Veteran's Ranch during the sixteen-week program for PTSD and living with a prosthesis, he turned on the light next to his bed and the white noise app on his phone, then started the breathing and relaxation exercises that had helped so much to calm his nervous system down. He wasn't reacting so far, and he hoped that doing everything he could think of to get ahead of it would help.

Laci knocked softly on his door. "Zack? Are you okay?"

"I'm fine."

"Are you sure? I saw your light on."

He could hear the hint of tremor in her voice and knew he needed to show her that he was truly okay. The Post-Traumatic Stress had gotten the best of him several months ago, and even though he had made huge strides toward recovery at the Veteran's Ranch, those closest to him kept a watch on him for relapse.

"Just a minute." He donned his prosthetic leg and walked to the door.

When he opened it, she was standing there with a blanket wrapped around herself and biting her finger like she did when they were kids.

She exhaled when she looked at him. "I couldn't sleep, so I was watching the fireworks from the living room window. When I saw your light go on and heard noise, I needed to make sure you were okay."

He wondered if people would ever stop worrying about him and if they would ever think of him as a normal person again. "I didn't mean to scare you. I guess you weren't thinking about what you were taking on when you married me."

She stepped forward and wrapped her arms around him. "You know I want to help you if I can. I couldn't help much when you were having trouble before you went to the Veteran's Ranch, but I can now."

"I'm really okay. I promise."

She looked into his eyes, as if trying to see into his head. "Okay. I don't want to bug you about it."

"Maybe I'll watch the fireworks with you. Do you mind if I bring the phone out and play the white noise app?"

She smiled in relief. "Whatever you need."

Sitting on the couch with her was far more helpful than the things he had been doing. Even though he wasn't having a flash-back, having her there next to him gave him a more tangible reminder that he wasn't back in a war zone and that all was well. For once, it was good that she was so distracting.

She reached over and grasped his hand. "I'm sorry I couldn't be there for you more when you first got back."

"I know. It's okay, you did what you could. I didn't really give you the chance, did I?"

"Not really." Her gentle smile reminded him that she didn't take it personally.

When he'd gotten home to Hideaway after his stay at Walter Reed almost a year and a half ago, he hadn't been much in the mood for company, and the last thing he had wanted was for her to see him like that. Between adjusting to missing part of his leg and the flashbacks, anxiety, and guilt, he had not been great to be around.

The only time he had left the house was when he went to work at Mitch's hardware store or to physical therapy. He had even put off the schooling he had always planned to start after his enlistment was up. A lot of days, especially during the weeks before he went to the ranch, he couldn't get out of bed, let alone the house.

His physical injuries were healing well at the time, and he was working around the prosthetic leg, even learning how to operate his specially-equipped truck. It seemed like the more his outside injuries healed, the more the injuries inside his head festered and grew. He felt like a failure who couldn't handle the memories and the guilt of surviving when he hadn't been able to save the guys who had died around him.

She had visited him at the store and come by the house when she could get out of her ex's clutches, but he had usually gently sent her away. When things came to a head for him and he went to a psychiatric unit in the hospital in Traverse City, then to the Veteran's Ranch, she called or texted at least once a day. She refused to let him push her away, and along with his family, she had been a lifeline to him.

She started giggling and nudged him. "You know, now that we're married and we're roommates, you can't send me away or stop me from helping you."

He shook his head in fake exasperation. "What have I gotten myself into?"

Her expression turned serious again. "Will you show me how to help you?"

He would need to warn her and explain what it was like when he had nightmares, but for the moment he was just going to enjoy sitting with her. He squeezed her hand. "This is helping, and I'm okay, really. I just wanted to get ahead of it. Plus, right now it's my turn to help you."

One of the hardest adjustments for him when he came home was the lack of mission. Laci and her baby were going to be his mission for the next several months, and he wouldn't let them down.

"You are helping me. You're a great friend." She looked down at his hand and fingered the wedding band. "And a great husband so far."

Husband. It seemed so weird to hear her say the word. They had never gone on a date before—not that he hadn't always wanted to—and now they were married.

He shook his head and stared at the ring. "Husband. That seems so weird. You're my wife."

When they looked into each other's eyes, they broke into nervous giggles. After a moment, the giggles turned into a long silence.

He didn't know what was on her mind as they watched the fireworks, but his was flooded with thoughts and questions about what was next. When they decided to get married a few days ago, they had only talked about doing what was best for the baby she was carrying and signing adoption papers. He was also focused on protecting her and the baby from her abusive ex in whatever way he could.

They hadn't talked about what marriage meant down the line. Neither believed in divorce, so as unreal as it seemed, this marriage was permanent. They would just have to figure it out as they went.

He looked down at her. While he had been lost in his thoughts, she had fallen asleep on his shoulder.

She looked so peaceful and beautiful. He would do whatever it took to protect her and the baby. Once they got through the months before the baby was born and then the adoption, they could talk about making their marriage more than a plot concocted by two friends to make an adoption easier and give a baby a safe home.

A glance at her lips sent his mind wandering back to the kisses at the wedding. He had no idea how he was going to get those out of his memory. Part of him wanted to remember and relive every detail, but that would only lead to more thoughts that he shouldn't be having. Since he wouldn't be sharing a room or any other marital activities with her any time soon, he needed to take all of his thoughts captive and lock them far out of his mind.

Knowing it was in his best interest to run from temptation, he carefully picked her up from the couch and carried her to her bed, then went into his room and locked the door.

Chapter 10

LACI COULDN'T SIT STILL in the adoption agency's waiting room a few days later. She had tried flipping through a magazine, but looking at pictures of happy people with their adopted children made her feel like there was a big hole in her gut.

She wanted to provide a safe and loving family for the baby and was certain that adoption was the only way to make that happen, but she didn't know how she was going to get through it. Zack was playing a game on his phone, but judging by his foot tapping, he was as nervous as she was.

She sat back down on the seat next to him. "How many people do you suppose base their honeymoon destination on where they found an adoption agency they liked?"

He chuckled. "We may be the first. Of course, we're also the first people I know who got married so that they could sign off on an adoption in the first place. You ready for this meeting?"

"As ready as I'm going to be."

A tall woman with a friendly face walked from the back hallway into the waiting room. "Laci? I'm Marianne."

Laci nodded as she stood and shook her outstretched hand, then gestured toward Zack. "This is my fr—my husband, Zack."

Marianne looked surprised, but recovered quickly. Once they followed her to her office and sat on the loveseat, Laci took out her notepad with the questions she had thought about after they had spoken on the phone last week.

The woman's eyes darted between them. "I don't remember you mentioning that you were married when we spoke on the phone."

Laci reached over and took Zack's hand, and he promptly squeezed hers. They were getting pretty good at looking like a couple. "We just got married a few days ago. You said that if we were married, Zack would be the baby's legal father and could sign off on the adoption, right?"

Marianne looked confused. "Yes . . . so you're married, but you're still looking at adoption?"

The question caught her off guard. Laci nodded and blinked away the tears that appeared out of nowhere. "Yes. We think it's best for the baby."

Zack seemed to sense her growing discomfort and put his arm around her. "We were hoping we could get things going with this today. She told me about your conversation the other day, and we're ready to move forward and sign any papers we need to."

Marianne's confused expression remained, but she spoke in a warm voice. "We're nowhere near the point of signing papers right now, so you don't need to worry about that." She handed them a folder with pamphlets about their legal rights and the process of adoption. "Laci, I know we went over some of this on the phone, but I need to go over it with Zack here too. There's a lot of information, and I want to make sure you both know everything you need to in order to make a final decision."

Laci looked her in the eye. "We've made our decision, but I would like to hear the information again, and I know Zack wants to hear it too."

Laci took notes while they talked, and Marianne answered all of their questions about the legal procedures. Laci was relieved that there was nothing mentioned about a paternity test and that they wouldn't have to go to court to sign their papers, but she was disappointed that none of the legal paperwork could be signed until after the baby was born. She had hoped they could sign something soon, thinking that if they signed away their legal rights, she could stop the growing feelings she was having for the baby.

She had felt love the instant she admitted to herself that she might be pregnant. Even though she had just broken up with Ronnie after a tumultuous two years together, she started day-dreaming about the three of them being a happy family. Certainly he wouldn't shove her around anymore if she was pregnant.

The dream soon turned to a nightmare when she told him she was pregnant and he immediately demanded she get an abortion. She was shocked that he would think she would do that and that he would be so casual about such a thing.

His callousness brought out her protective instinct and she finally stood up to him, telling him she would never consider it. When he backhanded her across the face so hard that she fell to the floor, her happy family daydream shattered and reality hit. It wasn't just her he was hurting anymore. Now he could hurt the baby.

She had stayed still and silent on his hard floor, thinking about her escape route. He towered over her as he called her a bunch of horrible names and said that it was her fault, then told her that if she didn't "take care of it," he would. Before stomping out of the room, he turned and accused her of cheating on him with Zack and said it was his problem to deal with.

When she left his apartment that day, she resolved to put the baby's safety and happiness first, no matter what. Her daydreams about being a wife and mother were replaced by thoughts about what she would need to do to keep the baby out of Ronnie's reach. She couldn't deny what he was capable of anymore and wouldn't put it past him to try to beat the baby out of her.

"Laci?"

She hadn't noticed that Marianne and Zack were both staring at her. It appeared that they were waiting for her to answer a question. "Sorry, my mind sort of wandered. I'm trying to take all of this in and think of any questions I need to ask."

"It's okay." Marianne's soft tone was reassuring. "I know it's a lot, but we've got seven months to make sure you both understand all of this. I was just saying that I would like to have a few minutes with you privately before we end today."

"Oh! Okay, sure."

Marianne probably wanted to ask more questions about what was happening with the pregnancy, like a doctor would. Zack squeezed her shoulder and gave her a sweet half-smile that melted her heart before leaving the room.

Marianne leaned forward in her seat and spoke gently. "I always need to meet with women without their partners present for a few minutes to make sure this is really their decision and they're not being pressured. Is this what you want?"

Laci felt tears stinging her eyes again and instinctively wrapped her arms around her belly, as was becoming her habit. "It's what's best. Adoption was my idea."

"Okay. Like I said, we have until the end of July to talk about that. One of my jobs is to make sure you've considered the option of parenting too. It's best to have those thoughts while the baby is in your belly instead of in your arms, so I'm going to challenge you to think about it, okay?"

Laci inhaled sharply. *No! I can't.*

Calming herself using one of the breathing techniques Zack had shown her, she forced a smile and nodded. "Okay."

"The other thing I need to mention while it's just the two of us is the topic of any other putative father. That just means assumed father in legal jargon. Boyfriends and husbands aren't always the biological fathers, and the court will ask you if there is another possible father."

Her head started spinning again. She focused on her purpose for being there. *You can do this.*

"Zack is the baby's father." It shocked her how easy it was to lie through her teeth to protect the baby.

She hoped God would understand and forgive her as she added to her lengthening list of sins. In every way but biology, it was true. Zack was the one who had just sacrificed his future to give her baby the stable family it needed, and it was Zack who had promised to help her choose her baby's parents. *Zack is the baby's father.*

Chapter 11

LACI FELL ASLEEP ALMOST as soon as they got into Zack's truck after they left the adoption agency. It was just as well, as Zack was lost in his own thoughts and didn't know what to say to make her feel better.

He hadn't expected it to be so intense sitting there talking about letting strangers raise the baby. Marianne had talked about the great families they had who were waiting to adopt and had said that there would be plenty of time to choose a family and even meet them before the baby was born, but something wasn't right.

He had a gnawing in his gut that he couldn't explain. When he and Laci had talked about it before, it seemed cut and dry—sign papers, pick a family, hide the pregnancy, wait it out, deliver the baby, and go on with their lives. Sitting there talking about how it would all go down and seeing the emotion churning on Laci's face while she tried to hold it together was a different story entirely.

It wasn't just the lying and secrecy of everything that didn't sit right with him. Adoption was great in theory, but any child would be lucky to have Laci for a mom. Had she considered raising the baby herself before she latched onto adoption as the only answer? Laci was smart and resourceful, and she loved kids.

She had probably thought about it but then realized that Ronnie would always be a factor. There would be no baby to raise if he followed through on his threats, and even if she had the baby, she would probably always look over her shoulder for him and worry about his interference. Yes, he was certain that she had weighed out all of her options and chosen the one that she thought was best for her baby.

Knowing that she had probably thought through every possibility carefully didn't do anything to quell the unsettled feeling. Had Mom gone through the same decision-making process when she found out she was pregnant with him? She had only been sixteen when she had gotten that news, not twenty-three like Laci, so she may or may not have. Even though they had started out with his father—never a dad, so he didn't get that title—they had left him when Mom decided she'd had enough of the abuse. That night was the last time he saw Kirk, which only confirmed Zack's sense that he didn't love or want him. Even as a second-grader, he'd been fine with that. He had just been glad to not always be scared and that he didn't have to hear his mom being hurt.

Zack had lived most of his life with a single mother, two wonderful grandparents, a doting aunt, and an uncle who was like a big brother, and he had never lacked for anything. Matter of fact, once his jerk of a father was out of the picture, he'd had a great life. Why should it matter if his father didn't want him?

There it is. That's what's wrong.

This baby might think neither parent wanted him or her.

The unsettled feeling had a name—rejection. He hoped that this baby would never feel that.

His phone rang, pulling him out of his thoughts. He scrambled to answer before it woke Laci up.

"Hello."

"Hi Zack, this is Callie from the apartment building. I'm calling with some bad news."

His gut clenched. "What kind of bad news?"

"Well, we had a pipe burst here last night, and the apartment you were supposed to move into tonight had some pretty serious water damage. I'm sorry."

"Do you have any idea how long it will take to fix?"

"Unfortunately, our regular contractor is out of town for the holidays and won't be able to start on it until next week. Once he gets in there and looks at it, we'll know more."

Great. Now they were homeless. His mind scrambled for a solution even as he absorbed the news. "Okay, thank you. Can you let me know as soon as you have a date?"

"Certainly. Again, I'm sorry about this."

"Not your fault. Let me know what you find out." He sighed as he ended the call and looked over at Laci, looking so peaceful even as she started to stir. *I can't even provide a roof over her head. How can I think I can be her real husband?*

She opened her eyes slowly. "What was that about?"

"Sorry to wake you. It looks like we're homeless."

Chapter 12

A FEW HOURS LATER, they sat at Cynthia's table after devouring one of her delicious pot roasts. She was an excellent cook, and Laci made a mental note to pay more attention to how she prepared the things Zack liked.

"Live here?" When Zack looked at Laci, she knew he was thinking the same thing she was. No one would be the wiser if they slept in separate rooms in the two-bedroom apartment they had planned to move into. If they took Cynthia up on her offer, or the others they'd received from Garrett and Mitch in the last two hours, they couldn't very well ask for separate rooms and keep up the pretense of being happy newlyweds.

Cynthia answered in her gentle way. "Give it some thought. I know it's not ideal for newlyweds to live in their parent's house, but the rent is cheap and it will give you a little more time to save for other things you'll need."

Wyatt took Cynthia's hand and grinned at her. "You know, Cyn, if you would marry me today, I could move in here and they could have my house all to themselves."

Yes!

"That's very funny, Wyatt. Just because these two got married in less than a week doesn't mean we're going to." A look passed between them that told Laci this was not the first time they had talked about their wedding date and Cynthia had reason to want to keep it at the end of March. Cynthia had stayed away from dating and relationships from the time she left Zack's father until a few months ago, when she and Wyatt had realized that there was more than a close friendship between them. Laci surmised that getting married, even to someone as wonderful as Wyatt, was something Cynthia needed to ease into. Her experience with an abusive ex was far worse than anything Laci had gone through with Ronnie, so it was not surprising that she needed time.

Wyatt threw his hands up in surrender. "Sorry, guys. I tried."

Zack pushed away from the table and started gathering plates. "Can we have some time to think about it?"

"Sure you can." Cynthia didn't seem to be upset. In fact, she seemed fine with them needing time to talk. "Actually, Wyatt and I were going to work on our own wedding plans, and we can do that at his house so you'll have some privacy."

Laci grabbed the serving dishes and followed Zack into the kitchen. They packed away leftovers and cleaned dishes in silence until they heard the front door shut.

She looked up at him. "What should we do?"

"It doesn't seem like we have a lot of options that wouldn't raise suspicions."

"I know."

"Your brother has the house all torn up getting it ready to sell, so there's a lot of noise to go along with the lack of privacy, and Mitch's spare room is the size of a shoebox."

The noise at her former home with all of Garrett's fix-up projects might trigger Zack, so that was out of the question. Mitch was doing some projects at his house, too, as he prepared it for his fiancée, Bella, to move into after their wedding in April. "Not a lot of options."

"I guess we're moving in here, then. I'm sorry."

She put her hand on his arm, knowing she would lose it if she hugged him. "Zack, this wasn't anyone's fault. We'll just deal with it and hope it's temporary."

They finished the dishes quickly, then Zack went to his truck to get their suitcases while she went into his room to familiarize herself with her new living space.

It felt so strange to be in there. She stood staring at his bed, which looked very small. If she thought it was hard to keep thinking of him only as her friend sharing the living room of their hotel suite for a few days, how was she supposed to manage sharing the bedroom that seemed to be shrinking around her?

He walked in and set the suitcases down on the bed. "All of a sudden my room seems so small."

She laughed nervously. "It's gotten smaller since I've been standing in here."

He pointed to a rug on the floor next to the bed. "There's plenty of room right there for me to sleep."

"No, Zack. You don't have to do that. It hardly seems fair that you wouldn't get to sleep in your own bed."

"It's our bed now. Actually for now, it's yours."

She was glad Wyatt and Cynthia had left so they could talk without anyone hearing them discuss their sleeping arrangements. Suddenly feeling woozy, she sat on the bed next to her suitcase. "This is so weird."

"I know. I'll call around to see if I can find a different apartment tomorrow, okay? Or maybe we could find a house to rent."

"Maybe." She thought about the trust Mom had left her when she died. Thanks to the academic scholarships that had put Laci through college, the fund had been gathering dust—and interest—since Laci was eleven. "I have an idea. Garrett swore me to secrecy about this, but now that we're married I can tell you something."

"Oh?" He paused in the middle of clearing out a dresser drawer for her.

"I have a trust account that my mom set up. Not the kind that I can buy a Ferrari with or travel around the world with, but one that could give us a down payment on a house or help with a mortgage payment."

He shook his head. "No, Laci. Your mom left that for your future. I know this might sound old fashioned, but it's my responsibility to provide a place for us to live. I'll figure something out."

Your future. Not our future.

She fidgeted with the zipper on her suitcase, feeling awkward. What was she thinking, talking about buying a house? Houses were permanent, and they hadn't talked about the marriage being anything other than a means to an end for the baby's future. She shouldn't have assumed that when he suggested they *get* married, he meant that they would *stay* married.

We may as well get this out on the table. "We haven't talked about it, but have you thought about what you want to do after the baby is born?"

"What do you mean?"

"After the court stuff is all done and you don't have to stay married to me."

He froze in place with his back to her. She probably shouldn't have brought it up, but she couldn't get it off her mind. He was as still as a statue and just as quiet.

He probably didn't want to show her how relieved he was. The least she could do for him was set him free after he'd done his duty.

Not knowing what to say or how to take his silence, she stood. "I'm going to go get a glass of water. Do you want anything?"

"No, thanks."

The tears that appeared when she thought of quietly divorcing after the baby was born surprised her even more than the ones at the adoption office.

Chapter 13

Zack woke up early with a stiff back and a headache. He made a mental note to find another comforter or something to add to the rug he'd slept on while he tried to stretch the cramps out of his muscles.

He donned his prosthesis as quietly as he could and got up to make coffee. Roscoe, his lab mix, met him at the bedroom door with his tail wagging.

"I suppose you're ready to go outside, huh?" He wagged his finger at him. "No barking."

Fat chance of that. Barking at nothing was his specialty. Zack slipped back into the bedroom to grab some jeans to put over his sweats, then put his coat on. After starting the coffee maker, he turned back to the dog. "Okay, let's go."

The early morning air was frigid, and he hoped Roscoe would do his business quickly without finding anything to bark at. Standing out in the cold air woke him up, especially his gloveless hands. As he rubbed them to warm up, he felt the wedding band on his finger.

Laci had made it clear last night that their marriage was temporary. He had gotten his hopes up when she mentioned looking for a house, but he must have misinterpreted what she meant. He shouldn't be upset about the idea of her buying a house and letting him live there while they were married. It might make him sound sexist, but he wanted to provide a home for her.

Now that he knew she was only planning on staying married for as long as they had to, he needed to work harder on not losing his head over her—as if he could go back in time and prevent that. His heart felt heavy when he fumbled with the ring and pictured the day he would have to take it off.

What did he really expect? Did he think the girl he pined after but never asked out would stay married to him when she didn't need to?

Before she told him she was pregnant and told him what a legal father was and he realized he could help her, he had resigned himself to the idea that he would never get married. Between his missing limb and remnants of Post-Traumatic Stress, he wasn't marriage material any more.

He had missed out on his chance with Laci because of his own cowardice, and now it was too late. Now he was married to her, but it was temporary. He didn't have any more chance with her than he had before she delivered the news of her pregnancy and took the til-death-do-us-part vow.

When he ushered Roscoe back into the house, Mom was walking into the kitchen.

"Morning, Mom. Coffee will be ready in a minute."

"I know you were looking forward to waking up in your own place this morning, but selfishly I'm glad to get you two here for a few days." She smiled and put her arms around him. "I know I should have been ready for it, but I wasn't prepared for you to move out quite yet."

"I know. Things changed pretty fast."

"I know you'll want to get into your own place as soon as possible, but you're welcome to stay as long as you need to."

"Thanks, Mom."

She made her way to the cupboard and pulled out the coffee mugs. "I don't know how this will fit into your plans, but Wyatt and I talked about it last night and he said that when we get married you really can move into his house if you'd like."

Zack chuckled. "He's already being a good dad."

"Yes, he is. He couldn't love you more if he was your dad, you know."

"I know. He's one of the reasons I didn't miss having mine around. Having him across the street for the last ten years probably changed my life." He kissed her on the cheek as he picked up the coffee pot. "And he finally stepped up and asked you out."

"It's funny that less than three months from now, you and I will both be married to our best friends."

He felt a stab in his gut. A few months after that, he would be divorced from his. He was glad he was pouring coffee so she didn't see the clouds forming in his eyes. He took his time stirring the cream and sugar into hers.

When he felt ready to fake newlywed happiness again, he took the cups and sat down.

"I always wondered why you and Laci never dated, you know. I wasn't going to be one of those mothers who tried to run their kids' lives, but I prayed for years that you two would get together."

His cheeks heated up and his lips curved upward. "I did too." No need to lie answering that one.

"So what took you so long, if I may be so nosy?" She winked at him over her cup.

"I was a coward. I figured being her friend was better than being nothing. I was afraid that if I asked her out and she said no, I might lose her altogether." He was never especially good looking and was always a stocky kid before the Army got hold of him. Laci, on the other hand, was one of the girls the other guys on the football team talked about in the locker room when they thought he wasn't listening. She was a cheerleader and could have had her pick of any guy in school. Luckily for him, they misread her shyness and thought she was stuck up, so she didn't date much.

He rubbed at the whiskers that were starting to itch on his jawline as he remembered all the times he wanted to ask her out but couldn't gather the guts. "I finally got my courage up a couple of years ago and was planning to ask her out when I came home on leave, but she had just started dating Ronnie. I wonder if I could have saved her a lot of pain if I hadn't been such a coward."

Mom leaned over and squeezed his arm. "We can't go back and change the past, honey. You've got her now and you can give her a good life. God has His timing, you know."

"I know."

"And now that you two have broken records for shortest engagement and courtship, should I be preparing to be a grandmother soon?"

When he choked on his coffee, she started laughing. "I didn't mean now, silly! You two take your time with that. Babies are a blessing, but they change your life. Enjoy each other for a while."

He was still coughing when he heard Wyatt knock on the front door. *Good timing.*

While she let Wyatt in, Zack poured his coffee then slipped out of the kitchen. His limit on talk about his marriage had been reached and it wasn't even seven o'clock.

When he walked into his room, Laci was lying in bed eating one of the crackers she had stashed in the nightstand. She was pale and sounded dead tired when she spoke. "You didn't have to knock, you know."

"I didn't want to startle you. Are you okay?"

"Yeah, it's just the morning sickness. It doesn't usually last more than a couple of hours."

Trying not to stare at her, he got to his task. "I'm just here to grab my clothes and head to the shower to get ready for work. Can I get you anything before I go?"

"Could I have some hot water for my peppermint tea?"

"Got it."

It was good to have reason to get out of the bedroom. Even though she was sick, seeing her lying in his bed with her curls going every which way made his mind wander to places it was better to stay out of—especially since she was planning on ending the marriage when the adoption was finished.

Chapter 14

LACI WAS GLAD THAT her job involved sitting. Managing the small office at the construction company wasn't exciting, but she was alone all day and she could sit when she didn't feel well. She had always enjoyed spending most of her day alone, but with the exhaustion that came along with pregnancy, it was suddenly a great gift. She could take a cat nap on the loveseat in the office when the others were at job sites, and sometimes did. She was counting the minutes until she was caught up on everything and the office was hers.

Her boss, Mr. Case, came in just as she finished clearing off the huge stack of papers on her desk. Being closed for ten days to give everyone a break over the holidays didn't stop the flow of incoming mail.

"Laci, I just came from the hardware store and heard a rumor about you. Did you get married, or were Zack and Mitch pulling my leg?"

She smiled and held up her hand, showing the simple wedding band.

"Well, I'll be. Congratulations. Zack is a lucky man."

"I'm pretty sure I'm the lucky one, but thank you."

"Don't tell him that. He lit up like a Christmas tree when Mitch said your name, so you've got him right where you want him."

She was sure her face was pink as she looked down at the invoices in front of her. *I wish.*

Mr. Case chuckled. "Looks about even then. If you would have told me you were getting married, I would have given you the rest of the week off for your honeymoon, you know."

She shook her head. "I would never ask for more time off after you were so generous with my limited work hours when my dad was sick and died last summer. And Zack had to miss four months when he went to the Veteran's Ranch for treatment, so he didn't feel right asking Mitch either. We think we'll take our honeymoon in late July or early August. Zack will be on break from classes then too." Could they really pull off a fake honeymoon while she delivered the baby?

"You two are a credit to your generation, Laci. Consider your vacation time approved." Mr. Case was a kind man and always reminded Laci a little bit of Santa Claus when he smiled. "Anyway, do you know where those reports for the planning commission went?"

"Right here." She handed him the folder he was looking for.

After sending him back out the door and spending an hour going through the mounds of mail, Laci looked at the clock. *No wonder I'm hungry.*

Just as she started searching in her desk for a bag of nuts, she heard heavy boots stomping outside and looked at the door in time to see Ronnie burst through it.

Adrenaline surged as she jumped to her feet, ready to dodge him and looking for an escape route.

"Laci! What did you do?"

In all the times she'd witnessed his rages, she had never seen his face so red.

"What do you mean?" She tried to hide her panic and act calm so he wouldn't notice her reaching over to her phone and tapping the SOS icon.

When she had broken up with Ronnie a month ago and finally admitted to Zack, Cynthia, and Wyatt that he had been rough with her, Wyatt told her about the Find 'Em app and added her to their family group. All any of them had to do if they needed help was tap the SOS icon and the others would receive an alert with location status. He was a policeman and he had instructed Zack and Cynthia, if they got an alert, to call him and stay put and he would respond in his squad car.

Laci scrambled to think of a way to buy time and to find a better place to protect herself and the baby from Ronnie.

His voice resembled something between a growl and a hiss. "You may be stupid, but you know exactly what I'm talking about."

She shook her head. "No I don't—*Ow*!"

He jerked her left wrist toward him to look at the wedding ring, throwing her off balance. She caught herself on her desk and managed to stay upright, but she was unsteady on her feet.

"You're hurting me. Let me go, Ronnie." Tears were stinging her eyes, both from the pain and her fear.

He didn't loosen the grip and it felt like he was going to crush her wrist. "You actually did it? You *married* him?!"

"Let go. That hurts!" The quiet and solitude that she once enjoyed in the empty office was putting her in danger now. There was no one around to hear her scream if she needed help.

Please Lord, let Wyatt be on his way.

Ronnie tightened his grip on her wrist and grabbed her other arm with his free hand, pulling her against him. "You little liar."

"I never lied to you, Ronnie—"

He shook her so hard that her teeth rattled. "Little church girl, always putting me off. You were messing around with him the whole time, weren't you?!"

"No, Ronnie, it wasn't like that—"

"Do you think I'm as stupid as you are? You're nothing but a lying little—"

He suddenly let go and she fell back toward the desk. She hadn't seen or heard Zack come in, but he was behind Ronnie with his arm squeezed around Ronnie's neck, pulling him back.

"Get your hands off her!"

Ronnie fought, but Zack's choke hold was too much.

"You think it makes you a man to beat up on a woman half your size?"

When Ronnie started to raise his foot to kick Zack's prosthetic leg, Zack threw him to the ground. Laci stepped behind Zack.

She grabbed her phone, but without taking his eyes off Ronnie, Zack said, "Wyatt is on his way. You're finally going to jail, Ronnie."

"I'm not going anywhere."

Ronnie started to get up, and Zack motioned to Laci. "Get back."

She did as instructed, hugging the wall. The scene playing out in front of her was unreal, more like a movie than real life. The voice coming out of her mouth screaming at them to stop didn't even sound like hers.

Ronnie got the first punch in, but Zack's sent him back to the floor.

Laci's eyes darted around the room as she looked for a place to hide. All she saw was movement. She crouched behind Mr. Case's desk and silently cried out to God to make it all stop and keep her baby safe.

Wyatt and Deputy Brody rushed through the door just as Ronnie got up and lunged toward Zack again.

"Alright, stop!" Wyatt's booming voice filled the room.

Deputy Brody grabbed Ronnie and with one smooth motion trapped his arms and slapped a pair of handcuffs on him.

Zack pulled Laci into his arms and turned her so she was facing away from Ronnie. "It's okay. I've got you."

She was still shaking. Something was wrong.

For the first time in her life, Zack's arms didn't feel safe.

Wyatt stepped forward while the deputy ushered Ronnie out the door. "Laci, are you okay?"

She pulled herself out of Zack's arms and moved back behind Mr. Case's desk, still looking for an escape route.

"Laci?" Wyatt reached out to her, but she backed away from him too.

Zack stepped toward her again. "Laci . . ." He stepped back out of arm's length, but held his hand out to her. "Will you let me help you?"

She nodded, but stood where she was, frozen in place. The only movement was the tears streaming down her face.

Wyatt's voice was gentle but commanding. "Zack, will you give us a minute?"

Zack hesitated, but quietly left the office. Laci couldn't look in his direction and moved back to her own desk to sit down.

"Are you okay, honey?"

She nodded without thought. She was nowhere near okay, but didn't know what to say to Wyatt. Her thoughts were a blur.

He walked over to the small refrigerator and got a bottle of water out and held it out to her. When she took it, he pulled a chair to the other side of her desk. "Do you want me to call Cynthia?"

She shook her head. "No, please don't tell her yet." She couldn't face her mother-in-law after what she had caused. Cynthia had taken beatings herself to protect Zack from them when he was a little boy. Laci couldn't imagine looking her in the eye after getting Zack into a fight.

"Okay. Do you want me to call a female employee at the station, or do you want to tell me what happened?"

"No, I'm okay. I'll tell you." She didn't even recognize her own voice as she spoke. "He just busted in here and started yelling at me about marrying Zack."

"Did he touch you?"

Out of habit, she started to shake her head, but realized she didn't have to hide or lie for Ronnie anymore. She slowly pulled up the sleeves of her sweater, revealing the red and purple marks that were already forming on her wrist and arm.

"Zack pulled him off me." Picturing the fight that followed, she felt sick. "It wasn't Zack's fault, Wyatt. It was mine. He was protecting me."

Wyatt shook his head and sighed. "You didn't cause this. Ronnie is a hothead and an abuser. As for Zack, I'm going to have a few words with him about interfering with police business, even though off the record I'm glad he protected you."

"He shouldn't have to do that." Laci put her head into her hands, feeling the weight of shame. "He shouldn't have to."

"Sometimes we do what we need to for the people we love. Zack loves you too much to hesitate if you're in danger."

No. He didn't sign up for this. I'm not really his wife. And now I've ruined him.

"Will you press charges against Ronnie this time?"

"Charges? But what if he—"

"I can have a restraining order on him by the time the sun goes down."

"He won't follow it."

"Then he'll deal with me."

Wyatt was a gentle man, but he was also a tough cop who had no patience for men who abused women. He had always been kind to her, but now he was less than three months away from being her father-in-law. She had no doubt that he would protect her.

This was all too much. It was her fault that she'd gotten Zack into this mess, and now she'd pushed him into violence too. And now Wyatt was involved.

She wanted to go home—not to Cynthia's house, to her childhood home. Knowing that Garrett would be full of questions and would want to do exactly what Zack had done, she knew that wasn't an option either. She wasn't going to make her brother violent too.

"Laci?" Wyatt broke into her thoughts. "I don't want to push you, but I need to get your statement."

She nodded again. "Okay. I'm sorry. Can I come to the station after work?"

The door opened again and Mr. Case rushed in. "What in blazes is going on in here?"

Laci stood to face him. "Mr. Case, I'm so sorry."

He held his hand up to silence her. "Are you okay? What happened?"

When Zack walked back through the door, she didn't know what to do. She wanted to both run into his arms and run as far away from him as she could get. Mr. Case was still looking at her, waiting for an answer.

"I'm sorry. Ronnie came in and—" Her tears took over and Zack suddenly appeared at her side and pulled her back into his embrace. She froze against his chest, feeling both protected by and afraid of the muscular frame he was holding her against.

"That's quite a shiner you're getting there, Zack. Did you get that defending your wife?"

"Yes, sir."

"Good boy. I've got an ice pack with your name on it." As he walked to the cupboard for the instant cold pack, he looked at Wyatt. "Sergeant Henry, if there's grounds in your investigation, I want to press charges against that punk for harassing my best employee on my property."

He handed Zack the ice pack for his eye and turned to Laci. "From now on, that door stays locked when you're here alone. We don't need any riff raff coming in and stirring up trouble."

She nodded. "Okay. I'm sorry again."

"Now listen. I don't want to hear those words out of your mouth anymore. That boy is nothing but trouble, and I know you didn't invite him in here. You go home and don't come back for a couple of days, you hear me?"

"That's not necessary. I'm okay, really."

"No arguing with your boss. Zack, go take care of your wife. Laci, go give your statement and I'll see you in a couple of days."

Chapter 15

THE SHORT RIDE FROM the police department was quiet, and Laci hugged the door and looked out the window the whole way. Zack was sure she wasn't seeing the snow-covered forests on the hills that she loved so much through that window.

It wasn't like her to be quiet, even under the circumstances. Zack had been heading straight home, but thought better of it. "Do you mind if we take a detour?"

"Okay." She sounded like she was resigned to whatever he said.

"Are you hungry?"

"A little."

"Me too. He interrupted my lunch." He stopped in front of the deli and within five minutes he was back in the truck with a bag of sustenance. Driving down Main Street to Hideaway Beach, he parked in a good spot for looking at the big lighthouse and Lake Michigan. There weren't usually a lot of cars there in the middle of the afternoon in January, and it might be their only chance for privacy. It also helped that it was one of her favorite places. They both loved seeing the beach covered in mounds of snow and contrasting with the steely blue lake.

She picked at her sandwich. "Thanks, Zack. I wasn't ready to face your mom yet."

"Why not?"

Her tears were back when she looked at him. "Because now I've gotten you into this."

"You didn't get me into anything. You know she doesn't blame you for Ronnie's actions." He reached across and gently touched her hand. "I don't either."

When she flinched, he wondered if he'd accidentally touched a bruise. "I'm sorry. Are you okay?"

"I'm okay."

You don't act like it.

She tucked her hand into her coat. "I know it's hard for your mom to see this kind of stuff, and I don't want her to have to see her son with a black eye and a cut up hand from defending me."

He chuckled. "Do you know what she would do to me if I let any woman—but especially you—suffer at the hands of a snake like Ronnie? Just because she taught me not to settle things with fighting doesn't mean she taught me to stand by and do nothing when someone needs help."

She just nodded and stared at the food she hadn't taken a bite of.

"Anyway, Wyatt just gave me an earful while you were giving your statement. This is on me."

"Why did you come, Zack? When Wyatt suggested the Find 'Em app, it was so you could send him, not get in harm's way yourself. Look what I've done to you."

"This?" He pointed to his continually swelling and discoloring eye and snickered. "This is nothing."

She wasn't deterred. "It's not nothing, and it could have been worse. You're not taking this seriously."

"You think I can't take him?"

"I saw you take him. That's part of the problem." The way she stared at his hands was unsettling.

She wasn't just upset about him getting hurt. She was afraid.

His heart fell. He leaned forward so she would have to look at him. "Laci, I'm not like him. I'm never going to hurt you."

She looked around as if she was thinking about jumping out of the car.

Panic started to rise at the thought that she would ever be afraid of him. "Do you believe me?"

"I don't know what to believe."

He took a slow breath before answering. "You know me better than that. I save my violence for slugs who attack women. Do you really think I'm going to let my best friend—my wife—get beat up by some low-life? I would do it again in a heartbeat, but I will never lift a finger against you."

Minutes that felt like an eternity passed before she looked up at him with eyes full of tears. "I'm sorry."

He finally got it. All the years of hearing his mom's story and the stories of the women she helped turned the light bulb on in his head.

"Laci . . . do you think that all of this is your fault? Not just today, but everything he did to you?"

Her tears spilled out. "He wasn't like that before, when we first started dating. He was really sweet at the beginning, and then he . . . became that."

"And you think you caused it—and now you think I've become that."

Zack set his half-eaten sandwich on the dashboard and leaned over slowly to pull her into his arms. He was thankful that she let him, but didn't like how stiff she was. "The worst thing he ever did to you was mess with your head to make you believe that. You know that you can't turn someone violent like that. And you know I'm not like him."

She finally relaxed into his embrace and held him too. He would show her or die trying.

Chapter 16

AFTER SPENDING MORE TIME looking out at the lake, they made their way back to Cynthia's house. The smell of Laci's favorite home-made cornbread and pulled pork greeted them like a long-lost friend. No one knew how to make comfort food like Cynthia.

Laci was relieved that Cynthia herself wasn't there when they walked in. She still wasn't ready to see her disappointment.

She couldn't stand to look at Zack's eye or hand. The guilt was too much, not to mention the swelling and blood. The least she could do was try to help him, since she was the cause of his injuries. "Can I get you another ice pack for your eye?"

"No, it's fine. I know you're tired, so if you want to go lie down before dinner, it's okay with me."

"Can I at least bandage your hand? Those scrapes can get infect-ed."

He shrugged. "If you insist."

She tried not to react to the way he was treating what happened. She was horrified at the scene and couldn't believe he would be so nonchalant.

Once she got his hand covered to her satisfaction, she headed toward his bedroom. "I'm tired and not really hungry. Do you mind if I just go to bed?"

"No, of course not. Do you need anything?"

"No, thanks." *I've done enough for today.*

"Laci?" He lifted his bandaged hand when she turned to look at him. "Thanks for taking care of this."

When she climbed into Zack's bed, she pulled out her journal. As she poured out her heart to God, apologizing for breaking Zack and ruining his life, she asked Him to give her a plan, to show her how to fix what she had broken. It seemed impossible at this point, but there was still that small part of her that remembered the verse that said that nothing was impossible with God.

She had just wiped the latest round of tears from her face when there was a soft knock at the door. Expecting Zack, she pulled the covers up to her chin. "Come in."

Cynthia poked her head in. "Forgive me for mothering you, but can I come in? I made you a plate."

She could only nod, taken aback by the kindness in Cynthia's eyes. Cynthia had always treated her well and been a friend to her, but she expected things to be different once Laci had gotten her son into a fight.

The tray that she brought in was loaded up. Not only did she bring dinner, but she also added a mug of mulled cider, a new box of tissues, and some magazines. She was amazing at comfort—so amazing that it added to Laci's guilt.

"Are you okay?"

Her tears returned. "Cynthia, I'm so sorry."

"Oh, sweetie." She set the tray on the dresser and sat on the edge of the bed, pulling Laci into a hug. "Please don't apologize. You didn't cause this."

"But I did. I should have just stayed with Ronnie. He was only on a rampage today because I married Zack. I got Zack hurt and I broke him."

"No, you didn't. Ronnie was on a rampage because that's how he is. He knows he doesn't possess you anymore, and he's angry about it." She brushed Laci's hair from her cheek. "We talked about this, remember? Sometimes they get more violent when their victims leave them. We should have predicted this and had some kind of protection in place for you, something more than just the app."

"I know, but now I've broken Zack. It's one thing for me to get hurt, but not him."

"Zachary's black eye and cuts will heal. He'll be fine."

Laci could only shake her head and cry.

"Laci, what is it?"

"What if he's broken forever now and I brought that out in him? What if he's going to be like his—?" She bit her lip to stop herself from talking. She shouldn't have said anything.

Cynthia rubbed Laci's hand as she spoke. "Zachary is nothing like his father. Are you afraid that because he fought with Ronnie, he's changed?"

She just nodded, remembering how quickly Ronnie had changed. How would she live without the gentle Zack she had always known?

"Can I tell you a secret? I've spent Zachary's whole life on the lookout for warning signs that he was like his father. There aren't any. He's a strong man, but he's also still the tenderhearted boy he always was. He looked like he was about to cry when he was talking about what it was like to see you hurt. He couldn't have stood by and let that happen."

"He was acting like what happened was nothing. It scared me."

"I think that's just Zachary being Zachary. He doesn't want you to worry about him, so he's going to act like getting into a fight is no big deal. He's not going to turn into a guy who looks for fights, and he's not going to turn into his father or Ronnie."

Laci nodded. "I just want my Zack back."

"Oh, honey. He's still here. He had to act the way he did to protect his wife." She leaned forward and lowered her voice conspiratorially. "Can I tell you another secret? He was afraid to come in here. He knows you can't look at him with his black eye. How about if I send him in and the two of you can talk? You don't want this to put a cloud over your brand-new marriage."

"Okay."

Cynthia leaned over and kissed her on the forehead. "Talk to Zachary and get some rest, okay? And let me know if you need anything."

Chapter 17

ZACK WIPED HIS PALMS on his sweatshirt as he walked into his room. He was relieved to see Laci eating the meal Mom had brought in for her. Roscoe snuck in behind him and jumped on the bed, snuggling up next to Laci and looking as if he dared Zack to try to move him. "Well okay, then."

She leaned over and kissed Roscoe and rubbed his belly. *Lucky dog.*

"How are you feeling?"

"Like I've been through a ringer today. How about you?"

"Like I've been punched in the face. How are your arms?"

She looked down at the red and purple masses where her wrists used to be. "Sore, but okay."

He stared at his feet for a moment, then sat on the floor next to the bed.

"My mom said you wanted to talk to me."

Laci half-laughed. "Well, she said we should talk and I said okay."

He chuckled. "She wants what's best."

"I know. I told her I was scared today . . . by you. That's what she wanted me to talk to you about."

I thought we covered this in the car. He scooted closer to the bed. "I really scared you today?"

She nodded. "I've never seen you get into a fight before. I never thought you could be violent. I was afraid I broke you."

He reached up and gently touched her knee. "Getting into a fight and being a violent person aren't the same thing. I fought Ronnie to get him off of you. I can't apologize for that, because I would do it a million times over to protect you, but I'm sorry I scared you."

"I overreacted. I'm sorry. I didn't mean to accuse you of being like Ronnie or—"

"Or my father?"

She nodded and looked down at her hands. "Or your father."

"Genetics aren't everything. I've got as much of my mom in me as I've got of him, and she's the one who raised me." He reached over and took her hand, careful not to touch her bruises. "I will never be anything like them. I promise. You know that, right?"

She nodded and sniffled. "Now I'm embarrassed."

"There's nothing for you to be embarrassed about. He put us in a bad situation today, and we did the best we could. Our bruises and cuts will heal, and we'll forget it ever happened, okay?"

"Okay."

They both turned when they heard the sound of a piece of paper sliding under the door. Zack went to get it and breathed a sigh of relief.

"Personal Protection Order, hot off the presses."

She didn't look comforted like he had hoped, so he set it down. "I know it's just a piece of paper, but it's something. He knows that if he violates it, he goes back to jail. Wyatt and I were talking earlier about what else we can do to protect you, and I asked Mr. Case if you could take Roscoe to work with you. He said he would feel better knowing that you had a guard dog with you at the office."

She looked at the dog and scratched him behind the ear. "This softie, a guard dog?"

"Trust me, if someone came at you, he would be all nails and teeth."

"He knows we're talking about him." She rubbed his belly, spurring Zack's envy again. "Do you want to come to work with me, boy?"

"Good, it's settled. I can also go eat lunch with you. Plus, Ronnie is spending at least one night in jail, so he'll think twice about coming anywhere near you again."

She reached down to him and hugged him. "Thank you, Zack. For everything."

Chapter 18

LACI WAS THANKFUL TO be back at work and to have something other than the confrontation with Ronnie a few days ago to think about, but she jumped every time she heard a noise. Mr. Case had installed a security camera above the door so that any activity outside could be seen on the monitor on her desk and no one could take her by surprise.

Roscoe stayed dutifully by her side and seemed to like his new bed next to her desk. Mr. Case even brought in a treat jar for him, so he was a very happy working dog.

When she noticed movement on the monitor and saw Zack walking up the stairs with take-out from the Bay Shore Diner, she ran to the door and flung it open.

"My hero! Ooh, do I smell chili cheese fries?" He probably heard her stomach growling all the way down at the hardware store.

He smiled and shook the bag. "After seeing the way you devoured the last batch, I bought two this time."

"Oh my gosh, you're the greatest friend—I mean husband—ever. I can't believe I never had these before and now I can't get enough of them."

"Hmm, if only someone would have offered them to you a million times over the years and told you that you would like them."

"Okay, I'll admit that you were right. The baby seems to love them too."

"The kid's got good taste."

She cleared off the corner of her desk, and they sat quietly scarfing down their lunches. His black eye was fading, but his knuckles were still in a bandage.

"How is your hand?"

He stretched it out. "The cut is healing up pretty well. I would like to see what his face looks like if my hand still looks this ugly." He looked around and leaned forward, as if he were telling her a secret in a crowded room. "I know you don't want me to be violent, and I promise I won't, but it was so worth it to finally deck that guy. And from what Wyatt says, I don't think we need to worry about him for a while. This wasn't his first assault charge, and the judge didn't go easy on him at the arraignment."

Laci still felt guilty for bringing Zack into it, but she shuddered to think what would have happened if he and Wyatt hadn't shown up. She rubbed her belly, relieved that the baby had been protected.

"How are your wrists today?"

She looked down at them and held them out. The purple marks seemed to be in no hurry to fade, but the swelling was going down enough to move the bad wrist again. "I'm glad I'm right-handed."

"I'm glad you're so good with your phone." He smiled at her as he dropped a fry into his mouth. "And eating chili cheese fries."

She smiled back at him. "I'm glad you're so good at getting takeout. Did you have a chance to call about any apartments today?"

"I called a few, but no one has two-bedrooms available for a while. I'll keep looking."

"Okay. I'm sure it will get easier being at your mom's. I just feel weird being there and making you sleep on the floor and lying to everyone."

"I hate lying, too, especially to her. Just remember we're doing it for a good cause."

"I hope they'll forgive us if they find out."

"They won't find out." He reached out and squeezed her hand. "And if they do, they'll forgive us. They'll understand."

Mr. Case walked in and chuckled. "My wife would swoon if she saw you two holding hands while you're eating lunch."

If only it was what it looks like.

Chapter 19

ZACK CHECKED HIS EMAIL on his phone as he walked into the house. It had been almost two weeks since he had started making calls and sending emails looking for a place to live, and there was still nothing available. The apartment that was supposed to be theirs was going to take even longer to be ready, thanks to someone's idea to do some remodeling while they were doing the repairs.

He was appreciative of Mom's generosity, but it was a struggle to keep up the appearance of in-love newlyweds while also keeping his feelings in check and thoughts pure. Every day it was harder to remember that they were only pretending to be in love, and every night it was harder to sleep in the same room with her.

When he walked in the door, he heard Laci and Mom chatting and working in Mom's sewing room. They had spent hours together working on projects over the past few months, and it had become a typical sound long before Laci became his wife and moved in.

Mom had used the excuse of needing Laci's help with a project for the Fall Festival a few months back so that they could spend some time together and she could encourage her after Zack shared his suspicions that Ronnie was abusive. Having lived through that herself with Zack's father, Mom had dedicated her life to helping other women get out and stay out of such relation-ships. He credited her with helping Laci to get strong enough to get out of the relationship and to stand up to Ronnie when he tried to intimidate her into an abortion.

When he walked into the room, Laci looked at him with hope in her eyes. As he leaned down to kiss her on the cheek, he whis-pered, "Sorry, still nothing." He grimaced when he got a muscle spasm while straightening up, and she looked at him apologeti-cally.

She had seen his pain over the last couple of days and had offered to let him sleep on the bed to help his back, but he refused. She followed him out of the room when he went to get Roscoe for his walk, and by the time he had the leash attached she had her coat on.

"What are you doing?"

"Walking the dog with you." It was hard to have conversations about things while living with a parent who worked from home, so they had been creative with finding privacy.

They were barely on the street before Laci started in. "We need to talk about our sleeping arrangements."

"No, we don't. I'm fine."

"You're not fine. You're in pain and I'm trying to help you."

"I don't need help." He walked faster, wishing she would just drop it.

Rather than dropping it or letting him walk away, she sped up to keep pace with him. "Why do you have to be so stubborn?"

"I'm not being stubborn."

"Stop sacrificing for me, Zack. You're making me feel even worse, and I can't handle it."

He stopped in the middle of the street to look at her. "I'm not sleeping next to you, Laci. *I* can't handle *that*, okay?"

"Why not?"

"Because I have my limits."

Her eyes widened as her hand flew to her mouth. "Oh!"

Embarrassed, he started walking again. He didn't mean to lose control and bring that into the conversation. He walked faster again, hoping she wouldn't follow.

She hurried to catch up with him. "I'm sorry. I wasn't thinking."

"I shouldn't have said anything. Can we stop having this conversation now?"

"How about if I sleep on the floor tonight?"

"How about no?"

"Argh! You're so stubborn, Zack Huntley." She turned and stomped back to the house.

He took the long route, wishing with every step that he was the strong, silent type. His mission was to keep Laci safe and help her with the baby, not to make her uncomfortable around him.

By the time he and Roscoe got back, Laci and Wyatt were putting dinner on the table. Zack and Laci both ate quietly while Wyatt and Cynthia chatted about their days over chili and warm rolls, and he wished again that he and Laci had their own place. He saw her looking at him out of the corner of his eye several times but kept his eyes on his plate. *You need to start keeping your lips zipped if this is gonna work.*

Chapter 20

AFTER CLEANING THE KITCHEN, Laci excused herself and went to bed early, claiming she was in the middle of a good book. She needed time to think. She wished she could pray, but since the day of the fight, she had been trying to stay out of God's way and didn't want to bother Him with the problems she had created.

She kept replaying the conversation in the street in her head. *What did he mean by that?*

He had made it pretty obvious that he didn't have anything but friendly feelings for her or want to make the marriage real, but then he threw that bombshell down. She remembered some of the comments Dad made about the differences between men and women. He said men had physical needs and women shouldn't get so wrapped up in things like feelings and commitment. Zack had never said anything about it, but maybe she was foolish in thinking that just because their marriage was in name only, there wouldn't be anything physical.

The idea threw her for a loop. She fought her feelings for him every day, and it was hard enough sharing a room and public displays of affection with him. Every time they stood with their arms around each other for the benefit of others in the room, she had to fight not to notice how wonderful it was to be in his embrace. The kisses at the wedding still haunted her, and she missed his lips. If they were sharing anything more than what they had been, how would she possibly manage when he eventually walked away?

Still, with all he did for her, she owed him. She was just going to have to try to separate from her feelings and give him what he needed. Love meant putting others first, and she would do just about anything for Zack.

She didn't know how to do what Dad said women needed to do. Separating the emotions and commitment from the physical act wasn't the way God designed things, and it seemed impossible. For her, the emotional part was there. So was the commitment. She would stay married to him forever if only he wanted to. The kisses on their wedding day had fueled her hope that he had the same feelings for her and the marriage could become real, but he was just being a good friend and putting on a show to help her out.

Maybe Dad was right, and she read too many fairy tales and romance novels. Maybe she needed to get with the real world.

It was time to grow up and be realistic about things for Zack's sake. She would talk to him about it when he finally came into the bedroom, and she would make it clear that she was inviting him into the bed for more than just sleep. It was the least she could do for him.

After touching up her hair and changing from the fuzzy pajamas she was wearing to the beautiful set Brianna had snuck into her honeymoon suitcase, she turned off the light and lit a candle. The darkness would both set a mood and hide everything about her that she didn't want him to see.

Once settled into bed, she broke her self-imposed rule about bothering God. *Please, Lord. Please protect my heart.*

Chapter 21

ZACK STAYED IN THE living room until he was sure Laci would be asleep. He was so embarrassed for blurting out what he did on the walk that he wanted to avoid conversation with her for a while. She had enough going on without that added awkwardness.

He hoped she didn't see him as some ape who couldn't control himself. The conversation was over anyway, so hopefully they could forget it happened. She was clearly not into him for anything but friendship, so maybe she'd forgotten all about it.

As he was turning off the light in the living room, the couch caught his eye. Since Mom was already in bed and he was always the first person in the house to wake up, no one would know if he slept there.

It was a great solution. He wouldn't have to face Laci and she wouldn't have to feel bad about him sleeping on the floor anymore. He grabbed a blanket and stretched out on the couch, which was far more comfortable than the bedroom floor.

The next morning, his back was feeling much better than it had every other morning, and the lack of pain made him think more clearly. He folded the blanket and put it in its usual spot and got the coffee brewing, then turned on the stove to heat water for Laci's tea before taking Roscoe out.

When he walked toward the bedroom with her steaming cup, he hoped she had forgotten the conversation in the street, and he was looking forward to sharing the brilliant idea he had come up with for their living situation. As long as there was a comfortable couch, they didn't need a two-bedroom apartment after all.

When he opened the door, his heart sank. Laci was sitting up with a blanket wrapped around her shoulders and up to her neck. Instead of greeting him with her usual smile, she met him with red, swollen eyes. He felt like his chest had just been kicked by a mule.

Closing the door, he rushed over and sat on the bed next to her. "Are you okay? Is the baby okay?"

"We're fine." She sniffled as she watched him set her cup down.

He took her hand. "What's going on? Why are you crying?"

"Because I'm completely failing you." The tears came out like a flood.

He reached out and pulled her into his arms. "What in the world are you talking about?"

"I messed everything up. I messed everything up for me, and now I've messed everything up for you. It's probably good that someone else is going to raise this baby because I would mess everything up for her too."

He had no idea what was going on. When she had cried over little things and blown things out of proportion, he'd chalked it up to hormones, but this was different.

Afraid to say the wrong thing and make it worse, he sat and held her for a few minutes until the tears seemed to run out. She clutched his sweatshirt as tightly as she had his arm during the wedding, but her shuddering breaths seemed to be slowing down.

"You haven't messed anything up, Laci. We're going to get through all of this. Together."

She nodded but avoided his eyes as she reached for the tissue box. Finally, she took a deep breath and her words rushed out in a verbal waterfall. "I'm sorry that I got you into this and I'm sorry that I kicked you out of your bed and haven't been meeting your man needs and I'm sorry that because of me you have to get into fights and lie to everyone. I'll bet you can't wait to divorce me."

"What in the—Laci, I don't even know where to start with all of that. You didn't get me into anything. Getting married was my idea, and so was sleeping on the floor. As for getting a divorce, that was all your idea, so don't put that on me."

Her eyes widened. "My idea— you don't want to divorce me?"

Not in a million years. "If that's what you want, then we will, but I want it on record that it wasn't my idea."

She looked down and fidgeted with the tissue in her hand. "We didn't talk about it when we decided to get married, so I figured you would want out as soon as it could be arranged."

No way on earth. "When I suggested we get married, all I was thinking about was taking care of you and the baby. I wasn't thinking about getting divorced, but if that's what you want, that's what we'll do."

"You said you didn't want to buy a house and that the trust was for my future, not ours, so . . ."

He took a deep breath. "Laci, you know what I believe about marriage and divorce."

The tissue in her hands was in shreds by the time she finally looked back at him.

This is your chance. Don't be a coward. "I don't want a divorce. I'll go along with it if you want to, but if that's not what you want, then tell me so we can start making this a real marriage."

She leaned forward and put her arms around him again. When he wrapped his tightly around her, she sighed. "I wasn't thinking about divorce when we got married either."

"So do you want to stay married and figure things out as we go?"

She nodded and looked up at him with a twinkle in her eye. "I do."

Her joke broke the tension and they laughed together. It was the first bit of normalcy in the conversation.

He squeezed her, wanting to dance around the room. "Okay, we're staying married then. I have one rule though. Please don't ever say the phrase 'man needs' again. I have no idea what that means, and it sounds weird coming out of your mouth."

She hid her face in his shoulder, and he fully relaxed for the first time since walking into the room. It seemed like something changed in that moment, and the way she had looked at him made him think there was a chance for a real marriage. Maybe she could even fall in love with him someday.

When she looked back up at him, the smile had left her eyes. "Zack, I'm serious about your needs, even if I said it weird. I've been hearing for years from my dad and Ronnie about men and their needs, and I want to be a good wife."

He grimaced and shook his head. Sweet, angelic Laci talking about men's needs in such a way made him squirm. "Can we please not use your dad and Ronnie as our standards to follow? I'm not going to say much about your dad because he was your dad and I don't want to speak ill of the dead, but Ronnie is a tool and I'm nothing like him."

"So you're not mad that we haven't . . . you know . . ." She lowered her gaze, looking like she wanted to hide.

He had to stop himself from laughing at how childlike she looked when she talked about such an adult topic.

"Of course not."

"I thought that was why you didn't come in here last night, that you were mad at me."

He couldn't believe they were having this conversation. "Look, I'm not going to act like I don't want that, but it would be pretty weird if we jumped into it when we just decided that we're going to stay married and we haven't even gone on a date. Let's talk about that when the timing is right and we're living like we're really married."

She looked down but not before he saw her red cheeks and her smile. He would do anything to get to see her smile more.

Even though they had just said they were planning on staying married, he was still nervous about asking her out. *Just do it.*

He lifted her chin with his finger. "Laci?"

"Yes?"

"Do you want to go on a date tonight?"

The surprise on her face quickly became a shy grin. "I thought you would never ask."

Chapter 22

LACI LOOKED AT THE clock on the wall, then her phone. Time had never moved more slowly.

She had finished all the invoices and billing statements that needed to get sent out and had organized the office while she waited for the time to pass so she could go on her date. Even taking Roscoe on a couple of walks during the day to make time move along didn't work.

Concentrating was difficult, especially when the texts that she and Zack had been sending throughout the day started taking on a flirtatious tone. Between the conversation that morning and the texts, she was starting to look at his comment in the street in a different context. It seemed that he just might have some more-than-friendly feelings for her after all. Thinking about that idea had kept a permanent grin on her face all afternoon.

Mr. Case walked in the door and looked around. "Wow, it looks great in here. Am I going to be able to find things?"

She laughed with him. "Of course! The phones were quiet and I couldn't sit still, so I finally did what I've had on my to-do list for a while."

"You're even more energetic than usual. What's got you so wound up?"

She couldn't contain her smile if she wanted to. "I have a date with Zack tonight."

"That's very sweet. Why don't you leave early? I don't want to get in the way of young love."

"Really? Thank you!"

She grabbed Roscoe's leash and almost ran out the door. When she got to Cynthia's, she greeted her quickly, then went to change her clothes for her date.

She rummaged through the drawers looking for something special. It was good that it was winter and she could cover up with sweaters. When she looked in the mirror, she looked almost normal from straight on. Zack had assured her time and again that what looked to her like her huge belly was not at all obvious, and at the moment he was the only one she was looking to impress.

"A-ha! There you are!" The pink cashmere sweater that Zack had always liked to touch was in the bottom of one of the bins she'd brought from home. It wouldn't hurt to wear something she knew he liked now that he had finally asked her out. She thought of all the times he had petted her arms when she was wearing that and shivered when she thought about him touching her now that they were flirting and talking about making their sham marriage a real one.

She couldn't help giggling at the thought that her husband might like her and had finally asked her out. He even looked like he was excited about it when they had parted ways this morning. When she thought of finally getting a real kiss from him at the end of the night, her stomach did a flip. She couldn't wait to touch those lips again.

Just as she finished touching up her makeup, there was a knock at the bedroom door. She opened it to see Zack standing there with a small bouquet of flowers and a big smile.

"Oh my goodness! They're beautiful!"

When he looked at her sweater, his smile got bigger, then he blushed. She hugged him and whispered, "Did you just check me out?"

"Mmm-hmmm. Now that I'm allowed to, I'm definitely checking you out. You look extra pretty tonight too. Did you know that's my favorite sweater?"

"Why do you think I'm wearing it?"

His grin matched hers as he stepped back and set the flowers on the dresser. "I hope you're not too hungry, because we need to make a stop before we go to dinner."

When they got into his truck and he pulled out of the driveway, he was still smiling.

"Are you going to tell me what the big smiles are for?"

"We may have a place to live."

"Really?" She clapped her hands. "Is that where we're going?"

"Yup. Mr. Ely was in the store today, and he heard me on the phone with an apartment manager in Traverse City. When I got off the phone, he said he had a small apartment over the garage at the back of his yard that we can rent for as long as we need it."

"Oh my goodness, yay! Our own place!"

"Here's the catch—it's only one bedroom. But after sleeping on the couch last night and waking up feeling great today, I realized we don't really need two bedrooms." He looked at her. "If that's okay with you."

"It sounds great. But after our conversation about staying married this morning, I thought we wouldn't be needing that second room forever anyway, right?"

He gripped the steering wheel and grinned, and Laci didn't miss the color rise in his cheeks. "Right."

Her face felt hot as she looked down. Realizing she didn't have to fight or hide her feelings and attraction anymore, she looked back up and studied him. The heat from her face wouldn't go away, and she found herself wanting to fast forward to the good-night kiss she was hoping for at the end of their date.

Before she knew it, he was pulling into the driveway. The place didn't look like much from outside, being just a standard apartment on top of a detached garage, but it could be *theirs*. She felt a little knot in her stomach when they walked up the stairs. She wanted to like it so badly and hoped she wasn't getting her hopes up too high.

When he opened the door, she squealed. "Oh my goodness, it's so cute!"

It was a small place and didn't take long to explore. The whole apartment consisted of a living room that was bordered by the kitchen appliances and counter on one wall and part of another, a bedroom, and a bathroom. The furniture had been around for a while, but was in good condition. Zack immediately tested the couch and gave it a thumbs up. Laci sized up the kitchenette and pictured them sitting at the small table and eating dinner together. The bedroom was bigger than she expected and had a small chair and ottoman in the corner that looked perfect for reading.

"What do you think?" He was looking at her expectantly.

"I love it!"

"He said we can use it as soon as we want. Do you love it enough to pick up a pizza and eat here tonight?"

"I love it enough to pack a suitcase and move in tonight!"

Chapter 23

ZACK HAD LEARNED HOW to pack a bag in under two minutes in the Army, so by the time the pizza was ready, they had their suitcases and a couple of boxes of necessities in the back of his truck.

Sitting at the small table with Laci seemed as natural as could be, and now that they were officially planning to stay married and even dating, he allowed himself to fully enjoy being with her as a beautiful woman. She was really his wife, not just his long-time best friend.

"Sorry this isn't much of a date. I was planning to take you to the Birchwood Inn tonight, but when Mr. Ely offered this, it seemed too good to pass up."

She stopped with her pizza mid-air. "Are you kidding me? This is a great date! You found us a home!"

"That's what I hoped you would say."

She touched his leg with her foot and winked. "You can take me to the Birchwood Inn tomorrow night."

"Gladly. Maybe you can wear that sweater again."

"Gladly."

She cleaned up the dishes while he brought the suitcases and boxes in, and they worked together to get the few possessions they'd brought unpacked and put away in no time. It was strange to think that the apartment they first set foot in less than three hours ago was already starting to feel like home.

He could see her getting tired and suggested they watch a movie on the couch, then looked at her sheepishly. "I guess in order to do that, we'd better get wifi or a DVD player set up."

"Oops. I guess we'll be holding off on movie night. Maybe by the time we get that stuff set up, I can get my popcorn popper from home—I mean my dad's house." She giggled as she sat on the other end of the couch. "This has been a really nice day. Well, other than my emotional breakdown this morning."

"Would I sound like a jerk if I said I was kind of glad you had that?"

"Probably."

It was such a relief to see her smile and sense of humor back. He hadn't seen it nearly enough over the few weeks since she got the positive pregnancy test.

"If you hadn't been that upset, you wouldn't have let it slip that you thought I was counting the days until I could divorce you and I wouldn't have found out that you didn't want to divorce me."

She cocked her head. "You really thought that?"

He shrugged. "I didn't know what to think. At our wedding, I kind of thought we were going to try to make a real marriage, but then I thought you changed your mind."

"I thought that at the wedding too. And I thought *you* changed your mind." She shook her head. "I guess we need to get better at communicating, huh?"

"I guess so. Maybe now that we're living alone and don't have to worry about being overheard, we can say words out loud and don't have to guess what the other is thinking."

"Maybe we can figure out how to be married without dating first too." When she laughed, her curls bounced along with her.

Sitting there with her like that gave him the courage he needed to put all his cards on the table. "Does it count for anything that I wanted to date you before but was too chicken to ask?"

Her eyes widened. "Really?"

"Really."

"That totally counts! Does it count that I always wanted to but was afraid you didn't?"

It was his turn for surprise.

"I'll be more bold about asking you out now that you have to divorce me to stop dating me." He laughed at the weird situation they were in and shifted on the seat. "Speaking of that, since you always wanted to date me and I always wanted to date you, come here."

She grinned and moved to his side. When he put his arm around her, she tucked herself into his embrace. She fit perfectly there.

"This is nice." She looked around, as if she was suddenly nervous. "You know, you were sort of bold at the wedding, the way you kissed me . . . I hoped you might do it again when you carried me over the threshold at the hotel."

"You did? I wanted to so badly!" He laughed and took her hand with his free one. "You mean we could have been doing this on our honeymoon instead of watching *The Office* in the hotel room and going to museums? I need to get better at guessing what you're thinking."

She got the signature Laci twinkle in her eye and gazed up at him, smiling. "What do you think I'm thinking now?"

His heartbeat thundered in his ears as he leaned closer. "Hopefully this." This time when he moved in to kiss her, it wasn't for a chaste kiss in front of a crowd of loved ones. It was the kiss he had dreamed of giving her for years.

They were both tentative at first, but they were soon fully consumed, as if they were trying to make up for lost time and opportunities. She convinced him with her kiss that she meant it when she said she wanted to stay married to him and make the marriage that started as a sham real.

It took every shred of his strength to end the kiss he had wanted for so long. He didn't want her to think he was trying to rush anything, and since her only experience had been with that creep Ronnie, it seemed best to move slowly.

He grinned at her as he held her. "Did I read your mind right that time?"

"Perfectly. I've wanted to do that since I realized you didn't have cooties."

"So have I."

Their lips came together again and it was somehow even better. Knowing his self-control was running low after several minutes, he drew back and rested his forehead against hers. "Suddenly I'm glad we don't have wifi or a DVD player yet."

"Suddenly I'm not in a hurry to get them."

Seeing how breathless she was made him want her even more. "I really like our new dating-marriage."

She grinned as she ran her finger along his jaw. "Me too. It's much better than our fake one."

"I don't want to rush you into anything, and I'm afraid I might if we stay here much longer. Can I walk you to your door?"

She giggled. "If you promise to give me a goodnight kiss."

"I promise." He stood up and took her hands, pulling her to her feet. The room was small so he walked slowly, not wanting the night to end even though he knew it needed to. "This was an amazing first real date."

When they got to the bedroom door, she turned to look up at him. "Maybe we should forget about the Birchwood Inn and have pizza and couch time again tomorrow night."

He shook his head. "Nope, sorry, no way—well, yes to the couch time—but I'm taking you on a real date with silverware and waiters first. Just because I married you already doesn't mean I can't court you properly."

"I can't wait."

He looked around their new living room. "I promise, tomorrow night will be more of a date than a moving party."

She put her arms around his neck and gazed into his eyes. "Every single thing about this date has been perfect. Thank you for finding us a home."

He hugged her goodnight and, knowing that the clock was close to midnight on his willpower, he stuck with a brief kiss at her door and turned back toward the couch.

Lord, give me strength.

Chapter 24

THE BIRCHWOOD INN WAS all Laci remembered it to be. The wood-paneled walls and the glow from the candles and fireplace made it the coziest and most romantic place she could imagine.

It had been years since she had been there with Mom, Dad, and Garrett. Their last visit there was to celebrate her eleventh birthday, the last one she had with Mom. She remembered seeing people on dates gazing at each other over the candles on the tables that night and hoping she could have a date there with her Prince Charming someday.

Wish granted.

Zack was a perfect gentleman, holding her car door and chair for her, ordering for her and remembering all of her special requests, and changing seats with her so she could be closer to the fireplace when she got a chill.

"You know, if I wasn't already married to you, I would definitely want to after tonight."

He puffed out his chest. "Is that right?"

"Yes, it is. You're a good date."

He laughed and leaned in as if to tell her a secret. "Already being married takes the pressure off the first date, doesn't it? Most people find out how people are on dates *before* they marry them."

"We're not most people."

"Good thing." Smiling at her, he picked up her left hand and slowly slid her wedding band off.

She gasped and tried to pull her hand back. "Hey, what are you doing?"

He held her gaze as firmly as her hand. "Trust me."

"I trust you more than anyone in the world."

"I know we've done everything in random order, but I want to set things right." He held the ring up. "Laci Kay Ryan Huntley, my life changed the day Mrs. Coulter sat us together. You made school my refuge from what was going on at home, and you've been my refuge ever since. I've loved you my whole life. Will you stay married to me?"

"Yes! I will—I do! Yes!"

He carefully placed her ring back on her finger and grinned at her.

"I love you, Zack." She squeezed his hand. "I'll stay married to you forever."

The waiter appeared at the table to take their dessert order. After the filling meal, they decided to share the chocolate lava cake.

"So, guess who called today?"

She couldn't imagine who and shrugged.

"The lady from the apartment building. The two-bedroom will be ready next week, and she wanted to know if we want it."

"We don't, right?"

He grinned at her. "I don't."

"I don't either." She raised her water glass. "To one-bedroom apartments and forever marriages."

"To one-bedroom apartments and forever marriages. I was thinking that with the deal Mr. Ely is giving us, if we stay there for a while, we can start saving for a down payment on a house."

"To houses. Houses are permanent and are for permanent marriages."

And for raising a family in.

Suddenly her mood bottomed out. Here they were, on a date and happily talking about the future, as if the baby in her belly didn't exist. Guilt consumed her, and she looked down to hide the sudden tears in her eyes.

"Laci?"

Her head felt like it weighed a hundred pounds when she lifted it to meet his gaze.

"Are you okay? We don't have to talk about houses if it's too much to think about now."

"Tell me we can have other kids to raise in our house." She tried to blink away her tears as he reached out for her hand.

"As many as you want."

When the waiter arrived at the table with their dessert, Zack asked for a take-out container and quickly shuffled Laci toward the door.

"You're a great husband, Zack. Thank you for getting me out of there."

Chapter 25

BY THE TIME THEY got back to the apartment and walked in the door, Laci's mood seemed to rebound. He hoped his words of comfort on the drive helped her realize that it was okay for her to have happiness despite the circumstances with the baby. It had taken him most of the time at the Veteran's Ranch to fully absorb the idea of being allowed to be happy in the midst of loss, but it had changed him when he did.

When he opened the refrigerator door, she grabbed his arm. "Hey, what are you doing with my dessert?"

"You just said you were full in the car."

"That's just my regular stomach. My dessert stomach is empty and wants that."

She laughed as she grabbed the container out of his hands and took it to the couch. He pulled two forks out of the drawer and joined her.

They still didn't have wifi or a DVD player, so Zack turned on one of the playlists on his phone.

"Dessert music. I like it." She took a forkful of the chocolate lava cake. "Wow, this is way too good."

"We'll have to make sure to order another one of those next time."

"Definitely." She looked at him with a sweet smile. "I'm glad you asked me out."

"Finally."

She put down her fork. "You really wanted to before? I thought you only saw me as your friend, and I gave up on waiting for you to ask."

"You really wanted me to ask you out?" He rubbed his face with his hands. "Geez. By the time I had the guts and had a speech prepared for when I was home on leave, it was too late."

She cocked her head, sending a curl tumbling onto her cheek. "Why was it too late?"

Oops. It had been such a great evening. He didn't want to bring up Ronnie's name.

He closed the container and set their forks on top of it, avoiding her eyes. "Uh, you were dating someone else."

"Who?" Recognition flashed in her eyes and her face fell. "No . . . Are you serious?"

"I'm sorry. Maybe if I hadn't been such a coward, you wouldn't have gotten hurt." He looked at her belly. "Or anything else."

She played with a piece of fuzz from her sweater. "I'm the one who chose to get involved with him. It's my fault."

"Hey. . ." He waited for her to meet his gaze. "We've both made mistakes. But now we're married and dating and living in an apartment that's all ours. We're going to have a great life."

Her attempt at a smile didn't convince him.

Chapter 26

IF THERE WAS EVER a reason to wish she could turn back time, he'd just given her the perfect one. If only she had waited a little bit longer for him.

"Zack, I'm so sorry."

"I am too. I wish we could have a do-over, but we don't get those in life." He had started absent-mindedly rubbing his leg, and she knew he was talking about more than the subject at hand.

"No, I guess we don't. We move forward and try to do better."

"Right." He reached out for her hand. "We're gonna go forward and do better together, right?"

The burden of her choices weighed on her. "Do you think we need to talk about some things before we move forward together?"

"Like what?"

"Like Ronnie."

The muscle on his jaw twitched. "You don't have to tell me about it if you don't want to."

She had only given him minimal information when she finally admitted that Ronnie wasn't treating her well. It was time. "I need to."

"Okay."

"I really messed everything up." She could feel the dampness already starting in her eyes. "Do you remember the teen Bible Club meetings at the beach?"

"Oh, yeah. They were fun."

"They were. Remember how much they talked about purity?"

He chuckled. "They definitely drilled that into us."

"They did, but I thought it was good. I always planned to wait for the perfect guy who loved God and loved me to come along, and part of that plan was to have my first kiss with him at our wedding. I promised God that's what I would do."

"I remember."

The tears were creeping up, but she needed to get through her story. More than that, she needed to tell it to Zack. "You know how things were when I went to college. My shyness got worse, and I had a really hard time making friends. I thought that if I graduated early like Garrett did, my dad would finally be proud of me, and I took such a heavy course load that I had to spend most of my time studying. Everyone else was out partying, but I was in the library or at church. That was where I wanted to be and I loved it, but when I graduated, it felt like I stepped into a black hole. I moved back in with my dad, and his drinking was so much worse. He never once said he was proud of me."

She wiped the tears that had slipped out from her cheeks and cleared her throat. "Anyway, Garrett was in Africa, you were off fighting in a war that seemed to have no end in sight, and the few other friends I had were still away at school. I had never felt so alone or lost in my life. When Ronnie came around, I was primed and ready for someone like him, as your mom would say."

Zack shifted in his seat, obviously uncomfortable with what she was about to say. She needed him to hear it, though, and could see that he was trying to be supportive. "He was really sweet at first, always telling me how much he liked being with me. He wanted to be with me every spare moment and called and texted constantly when we were apart. I took it as him falling in love with me, not as the possessiveness that it was."

Not wanting to drag the story out longer than she needed to, she tried to get to the point. "After a while he started pressuring me and started making jokes about my vow to God. When I look back now, I can see how the jokes got more cutting little by little and how he slowly backed off on the compliments unless they were the backhanded kind."

Zack's jaw was set and face taut, but he continued listening. Even if she wanted to, she couldn't stop her story. The floodgates that she had kept locked for two years were open, and there was no going back.

"He kept saying that we were going to get married eventually, so it wouldn't really be breaking the vow I had made. I was still giving my first kiss to my husband, just not at the wedding. Plus, he said he had to know if we were compatible before he could marry me. When I finally gave in to kissing, he upped the pressure about other stuff and said anything we did was still okay because we were going to get married. He went on and on about how men have needs and started accusing me of hurting him if I didn't give him what he needed."

Zack's face was getting red, and she could tell that he was doing his breathing exercises to stay calm.

"I'm sorry. I didn't mean to upset you."

"I'm not upset at you, Laci. I'd just like to punch him again right now." He put his hands up as if surrendering. "I know, I know, I won't do it, I promise. Go ahead."

"Okay. I finally gave in. I thought that maybe if I gave him what he wanted, he would start being nice again. My vow to God was shattered with that first kiss, and I figured what did it matter at that point? I was sure that God was ashamed and disappointed in me, and I thought I could never make it up to Him. I just stopped trying."

She could see him biting his lip and figured she'd better wrap it up.

"I guess that's it for now. Sorry for spilling all of this on you. I just needed you to know that I didn't just change."

"I never thought you did. And you know that I had my time when I wandered from what I knew was right too. I didn't wait for our wedding for my first kiss either. And I didn't wait for— well, I didn't make as strict a vow as you made, but I broke the one I made too."

She remembered back when he told her that. She had never been so jealous in all her life as she was of Zack's girlfriend who got to share that with him. "How are we going to try to make it up?"

"We can't. That's what forgiveness is for. We messed up and God knows we're sorry and that if we could change it, we would."

"I'm trying."

"I know." He shifted in his seat. "Aren't you missing something in your story?"

She wanted to stop talking. She couldn't stand to see the tension on his face. He had to be just as disappointed in her as God was and as Mom would be even though he wasn't saying it.

"Do you want to tell me about when he started hurting you?"

She sighed. He was already angry after hearing about Ronnie pressuring her. How would he react to hearing about him hitting her?

Ronnie was right. She talked too much. She never should have started this conversation.

Zack reached over and stroked her hand. "I'm sorry, I don't mean to push you. I know it was hard to tell me what you just did."

"I'm sorry I brought it up. I was only thinking of myself, and I know it's hard for you to hear it."

"I can take it, Laci. I was there when Kirk was violent, remember? The only reason he didn't beat me was because my mom stood in the way and took it for me. It's hard for me to hear, but I want to listen if you need to talk about it."

She felt the tears coming, picturing Zack as a frightened little boy. He wasn't a little boy anymore though. He was a man who had already shown the lengths he would go to in order to protect her. What would he do to avenge her?

"It doesn't matter now. It's over. I don't want you to be upset or . . ."

He reached over and gently tipped her chin up. "I'm not going to go out and give him the pounding he deserves. I told you I didn't turn into a violent person, and I meant it. When I fought him, it was to get him away from you. Let me prove it to you."

Zack had never broken a promise to her in all the years they had been friends. He wouldn't start now.

"It wasn't that bad, really—not as bad as what your mom went through. I never broke any bones or had to go to the hospital or anything. He just got a little rough when we argued." She shook her head. "I shouldn't have talked back to him. It was as much my fault as his."

"Laci, *no.*"

She jumped at his sharp tone. *Just stop talking. You're asking for it again.*

Zack's face was soft, but his eyes were intense. "You've argued with me our whole lives and you argue with Garrett. Have either one of us ever hit you?"

"No, of course not."

"That's because we're not the kind of scumbags who hit women. You can't turn someone violent."

She nodded, looking down at her hands.

"Come here. Please?" His tone and eyes were gentle as he held his arm out in invitation. "Please?"

She slowly moved toward him, and he pulled her into his arms. His strength made her feel safe and protected. Everything she went through with Ronnie was over, and she was finally with the right man.

"You don't have to cover up for him anymore, and it wasn't your fault. You don't have to tell me the rest right now, but you don't have to hide it from me either, okay?"

As she nodded, the tears rushed out from somewhere deep inside. The emotions she felt were so jumbled that she didn't have names for them. Zack was telling her she wasn't to blame though. She knew God was telling her to listen. Maybe they weren't as disappointed in her as she thought. She was crying so hard that she couldn't hear the soothing words he was saying as he held her tightly and stroked her back.

She had never felt so comforted in her life.

Chapter 27

ZACK TRIED BUT FAILED to stay out of his own thoughts as he held Laci. He hated to see women cry. Mom had always tried to hide her tears from him, but there were many times that he had heard her muffled sobs behind her bedroom door when something happened that brought up old memories of his abusive father.

Laci had denied any abuse when he had asked her directly a few months ago, and she had even kicked him out of her house and stopped taking his calls for a week. She finally came around again, but didn't admit that Ronnie had gotten physical until after she broke up with him. Even then she had been vague and downplayed it, but he could tell by her actions that it had been happening for a while. Spending time with veterans who had gone through trauma and going through it himself, he knew the signs well.

Not knowing what else to do, he held her tightly and told her he loved her. The last time she cried with such abandon was the day after Christmas when he stopped by her house unannounced and she met him at the door with red eyes and a swollen cheekbone. He had held her just like this, and when she calmed down enough to speak, she told him she was pregnant. Searching for solutions to help her and stop the tears, he had suggested the marriage.

These tears seemed different than the ones she shed that day. Tonight it seemed like release, like letting go.

Laci's sobs quieted and she went slack in his arms. He held her there for several minutes while he prayed for her.

When her breathing sounded like that of deep sleep, he carefully stood and carried her to bed. He hoped she wouldn't have nightmares like he and Mom sometimes did, but he wanted to be nearby in case she did. Once he got her tucked in, he retrieved the blankets from the living room and got as comfortable as he could in the chair in the corner of the bedroom.

He couldn't prevent her nightmares any more than he could prevent his own, but he could stand watch over her and be ready if she needed him.

When Zack woke up the next morning, Laci was still sleeping. He got out of the chair slowly, partly because he didn't want to make a sound to wake her and partly because he was stiff all over. A hot shower would rid him of the knots in his muscles. If only it would rid him of the memory of what she'd told him and the pictures he now had in his head.

He didn't know which image was worse—the one of her being hurt or the one of her in Ronnie's arms. Each one had its own way of punching him in the face.

When he walked out of the bathroom after a long shower, she was in the kitchen area making coffee for him while her tea kettle heated.

"You don't have to do that, but thank you."

"You take care of me, I take care of you." She smiled and accepted the hug he offered.

It felt good to hold her and to see that she seemed better. "Did you sleep okay?"

"I did. I guess a good cry and a soldier sleeping in the chair are great sleep aids."

"You saw me?"

"I saw you." She gave him an extra squeeze. "Thanks."

He leaned his cheek against her hair. "I wanted to be there in case you had nightmares."

"I know. When I saw you there in the middle of the night, that was what I figured. I know how hard it has always been on you when that happened to your mom."

"Do you feel better?"

"Yeah. That was the first time I talked about it, so it kind of gushed out of me. Thanks for listening."

He lifted her chin up to look into her eyes. "Thanks for trusting me with it."

Chapter 28

LACI'S MORNING DRAGGED ON almost as much as yesterday. The phones were busier, but she still had a lot of free time to fill, and she and Roscoe worked through her to-do list. She saw activity on the security video and ran to the door when she saw that Garrett had brought lunch to her.

"Garrett!" She almost crushed the bag in his hand with her hug, but he moved it just in time.

"Careful with the food, Laci Lou. Priorities!" He grinned at her and kissed her on the cheek. "Your husband was unavoidably detained because of some delivery at the hardware store and said you might like to have lunch with me."

"I'd love to have lunch with you. This is a great surprise!"

"That's very sweet that he comes over and has lunch with you every day." He set the bag on the end of her desk and shrugged off his coat while she cleared a spot for their food. "Does that have anything to do with the new security cameras and a certain rumor I heard?"

Oh no. She tried to think of something to say. Zack had promised not to tell, but it was a small town. It was inevitable that Garrett would hear about it.

"Laci, why didn't you tell me? Are you okay?"

"I'm okay. Ronnie was just mad because I married Zack and he came in here to yell at me about it."

The concern on Garrett's face was clear, and she knew he wasn't buying her casual recounting of events. "From what I heard, there was more than yelling. Did he hurt you?"

"I'm okay. Zack got him away from me before he could do much." She unconsciously stroked her belly under her desk.

"You found yourself a good husband. And from what I heard, he's got an effective right hook."

"Yeah, well, that's the last thing I wanted to happen."

Garrett shifted in his seat. "I guess since you're away from Ronnie and you know that I know about the other day, I can ask. This is what was going on with him last summer, wasn't it? This is what you weren't ready to talk about when I asked?"

She didn't want Garrett to storm over and start something with Ronnie, so she had thought it best to keep it to herself. How wrong she was. If she would have gotten away from Ronnie then . . . "Enough about me. How are you and Brianna?"

Garrett grinned at the sound of Brianna's name, but quickly got back to the conversation he seemed intent on having. "Nice try, little sis. We're great. Back to you. Is this the thing you didn't want to talk about after Dad died?"

"I don't want you confronting Ronnie, Garrett. It's over and he's out of my life. I've even got a restraining order and a guard dog."

Roscoe humphed from under the desk, as if confirming her story.

"I'm not going to do anything. I'd like nothing more, but I'm not going to." He took a swig of his Coke. "I've suspected this was going on since then, Laci. If I was going to pop the guy, I would have done it months ago."

"Why didn't you?"

"Because Brianna told me that would make you defend him and make you more bonded to him or something like that."

Her eyes grew wide. "Brianna knew too?"

"She was trying to help me help you. A lot of good it did." He shook his head. "I'm just glad you're out of that relationship and finally with the guy you should have been with all along. How's the honeymoon going?"

Her grin apparently gave him his answer.

"Good for you. I was happy to give you away to him."

She swatted at his arm. "Hey!"

He moved out of the way before she could make contact and snickered at her. "I didn't mean it that way. I meant that I wouldn't have given my blessing if you'd tried to marry anyone else on two days' notice."

"It was five days." She stuck out her tongue at him. "Really, though, thanks for not giving us a hassle about such a short engagement."

"To be honest, I was afraid you would go back to Ronnie, so I was glad Zack got you down the aisle before you could change your mind."

Wow. Her brother was full of surprises today. "Well, I didn't change my mind, and I never will. I've wanted to marry Zack for most of my life."

"What?" His jaw dropped. "Why did you act like you were just buddies?"

"Because he didn't act like he liked me that way. He just told me the other day that he always wanted to ask me out but was afraid I would say no."

"Well, I'm glad you two finally got your act together. When are you going to make me an uncle?" He winked as he shoved the last bite of his sandwich into his mouth.

"Garrett!"

He laughed at her, clearly enjoying making her uncomfortable. "I think I'll make an awesome uncle, and I want to practice on your kids. You know, to work the kinks out."

She felt her cheeks warm at his teasing. "Stop it!" His grin brought out her own. "When are you going to marry Brianna and make me an aunt? You know I'll be great at that."

It was nice to be able to laugh with Garrett again. The months he had been home since leaving the mission field were mostly filled by going through Dad's illness and death and dealing with his estate. They hadn't had a lot of time to tease and laugh.

"Soon enough. Sorry to eat and run, but I've got to go meet your crew at the house." He stood and pulled his coat from the back of his chair. "Tell Mr. Case thanks again for giving us your employee discount on the bathroom renovation. The realtor said it's going to make a big difference when we finally get it on the market. That is, if you're sure you and Zack don't want to move in."

She shook her head. "You and I agreed we didn't want to live there with all those bad memories, Garrett. Let's get it sold."

"That's what I thought, but I wanted to make sure." He zipped his coat and walked toward the door.

"Garrett?"

"Yeah?"

She walked over to him and put her hand on his arm. "It did help."

He looked at her quizzically.

"I knew you and Brianna were spending a lot of time with me after Dad died to help me even though I thought you didn't know what was going on. You helped me get stronger even though you didn't know it."

He gave her his best big brother bear hug. "I love you, Laci Lou. I would do anything for you."

When he opened the door to walk out, she called after him, "Then make me a bridesmaid!"

Looking down at her belly, she thought better of that. She didn't know how she was going to hide it in Cynthia and Wyatt's wedding in a couple of months. When Garrett and Brianna got engaged, she hoped they would take a good long time to plan their wedding.

Maybe she would suggest they elope.

Chapter 29

ZACK AND LACI SAT together on the couch after dining on takeout from Anchor's. He hadn't gotten a break all day and was starving when he left work, so the rib basket was practically calling his name.

Laci nudged his foot. "Thanks for dinner. And for sending Garrett to have lunch with me today. It was nice to spend time with him."

"I'm glad he was available. The delivery truck driver said they were late on their whole route because of that snowstorm that hit Chicago, and I didn't want you and the baby starving to death."

Her brow furrowed. "You didn't tell Garrett about what happened with Ronnie, right?"

"Nope. I told you I wouldn't."

"Well, he knows. He also let it out that he and Brianna knew something was going on with Ronnie last summer."

We all did. Zack cocked his head, wondering if he should tell her.

She sat up and looked at him. "You talked to him, didn't you?"

"Not about the other day." Her silent stare let him know she knew he was holding something back. "We may have talked about our suspicions last fall. We were worried about you."

She slumped back in her seat. "Part of me isn't happy that you were all talking behind my back."

"Is the other part of you happy that people love you enough to be concerned and want to protect you?"

She paused, then smiled and returned to her spot snuggled against him. "Actually, yes."

"Good. It was awful not being able to say anything to you, but my mom and Brianna both said it would make things worse."

"Your mom knew too?" She sat up again, looking him square in the eye. "Wait, is that why she begged me to help her sew the hats and aprons for the Fall Festival?"

"Well . . . she did need help, but she also wanted to help you. We thought maybe you would talk to her." He hoped she wouldn't be mad.

"That's why she kept talking about your father. Now I feel stupid."

"Because people wanted to help you?"

"No, just . . . I don't know."

"My mom loved having an excuse to hang out with you. She's always liked you and wanted us together, even though I didn't know that part."

"But she didn't really need help?"

"No, she did need the help. Evelyn and Mrs. Stevens offered to help her, but she wanted to do it with you. I could tell she was having fun with you and liked teaching you. She was really excited when you moved on to making your own clothes."

Laci sat quietly.

"She had fun with you." He reached down to her side and tickled her. "Everyone has fun with you, Bubbles."

She giggled at her old nickname. "Are you ever going to tell me why you call me that?"

"No." Now he was laughing.

"Why not?"

"Because it should be obvious."

"Maybe not to me."

He groaned, enjoying teasing her just a bit longer. "Fine. Remember when Mrs. Coulter put us at the same table? The shy girl and the quiet boy?"

"Yes. That's when I started liking school."

"Me too. Remember when you wouldn't sit still and she said you had ants in your pants?"

"Yeah . . . wait a minute! You said I didn't have ants in my pants, I had bubbles in my blood!"

He couldn't control his laughter, picturing the little girl with her blonde curls bobbing up and down when she got excited. "You still have bubbles in your blood, you know."

"I guess that does sound a little better than ants. You have a nickname too—well, sort of."

"What does that mean?"

"I changed your name to Zelda in my phone so Ronnie wouldn't know it was you I was texting with."

"Zelda! Now I'm a Viking princess or something?" *Horrifying. Absolutely horrifying.*

She giggled. "I couldn't think of anything else and had to do it quickly. So you were Zelda."

"Zelda . . ." He shook his head.

"Ronnie was so jealous of you that he would flip when he knew we were talking, so I gave you a girl's name."

Knowing that she deceived Ronnie so she could talk to him felt good. So did the fact that she got away with something under Ronnie's controlling nose. "Am I Zack now?"

She picked up her phone from the coffee table in front of them and showed him. "Satisfied?"

"Very. I don't want you thinking of me as a Viking princess. I want to be a manly man."

"Oh, you are. You're my manly prince—no, my knight in shining armor." She leaned up and kissed him on the cheek, then started fidgeting with her sweater again. "Can we go back to part of our conversation last night?"

"That depends. Which part?"

"The part where you said you always wanted to marry me. Is that true?"

"One hundred percent."

She leaned her head on his shoulder. "Good. I like that part."

Chapter 30

LACI LOVED THE NEW apartment. Even though they had only been there for two weeks, it felt like home. After adjusting the curtains she had just hung, she nodded, satisfied with her work.

She had made the curtains and throw pillows from some coordinating fabrics she'd found on sale on her last trip to the fabric store in Traverse City with Cynthia, and she couldn't wait to surprise Zack with the new look. She had worked on them at Cynthia's house when Zack was studying or working late at the hardware store, and she and Cynthia were both sure he would like the new décor.

When Zack walked in the door, she greeted him with what was now her standard hug and kiss. "Well, what do you think?"

He looked around the room. "What's different?"

"Seriously? You don't notice?" *Men.*

He looked around again, bewildered. "You look pretty."

"Nice try. The curtains? The pillows?"

He looked again, this time taking in the new additions. "Oh! Nice! I like the fabric."

She bobbed in her excitement. "I wanted to do something to make it feel more like ours since we didn't choose the furniture or anything."

"I love it. Thanks for not making it too girly in here." He leaned down and kissed her cheek, which was also becoming a habit.

She was definitely enjoying acting like a married couple even when no one was around. Well, at least like a dating couple.

"It smells delicious in here. Thanks for making dinner."

"I think I'm becoming an expert in crock pot cuisine."

He set the table and carried over the plates with the chicken and rice dish she'd experimented with. "This looks great."

As he prayed for the meal, she felt like her chest was going to burst from gratitude. She didn't know how God had given her such a good man after she had messed up, but she was learning to accept grace when it was given.

She didn't like talking about the baby or the adoption much, so she wanted to get the discussion about her conversation with the adoption agency over with. "I talked with Marianne today."

"Did you make another appointment for us?"

"Yes, she said Wednesday worked for her too. She asked if we've talked about parenting."

His jaw dropped and he set his fork down. "Really?"

Laci nodded. "She's brought it up before and said that especially because we're married, she wants us to be sure to talk about it while I'm still pregnant. I think she's afraid we're going to change our minds." She fidgeted with her fork to hide the moisture in her eyes. "Anyway, I lied and said we had and that we still think adoption is the best choice. If I tell her that keeping the baby isn't an option, it might raise questions."

He nodded and stared at the wall, appearing lost in thought. "Do you think about it? Raising the baby?" When he looked back at her, his eyes had a look she couldn't read in them.

"That wasn't part of our agreement. You didn't sign on to be a father to another man's child. I can't really ask you to consider it, and I can't consider it myself." She wanted the conversation over.

He rubbed at his chin. "I think she's right. We do need to talk about it."

She was stunned. She didn't know what she had expected or wanted him to say, but she didn't think it would turn into a discussion about keeping the baby. It was too much.

Tears filled her eyes. "I don't think I can talk about it. I don't even want to think about it."

He reached out and took her hand. "I don't want to think about it either, but I can't always stop the thoughts. Sometimes I dream about him."

"Me too. I think it's a her though. This would be easier if I could think of her as an it."

"I know. I keep picturing the ultrasound picture in my head though. That's definitely a him or a her." He took a deep breath. "What do you really want?"

Her tears spilled over. "I want what's impossible. I want the baby to be yours."

Chapter 31

ZACK WATCHED THE SNOW falling on Main Street from the warmth of the hardware store. He was glad the storm had given them reason to cancel the appointment they had scheduled at the adoption agency for tomorrow. Since they hadn't talked about the possibility of parenting like Marianne had asked, he was afraid of what questions the woman would ask when they did see her. Laci still wasn't ready to talk about the idea of raising the baby as theirs, and he was probably even less so.

He knew it *was* real, but it didn't *seem* real. The time was coming when it would, but he was in no hurry to push it. It was easier to talk with Laci about it when it was only real—and therefore emotional—for her. If he could keep some distance, he could help Laci to think about it and be sure of what she wanted.

He heard the bell on the door jingle and looked up from the shelf he was stocking to see Joe and Emily Callahan walk in with their daughter, Lily. He shook his head and rolled his eyes toward heaven.

That's very funny. I'm trying not to think about pregnancy, and the most pregnant woman in Hideaway walks into the store. I want it on record that I'm not always crazy about Your sense of humor.

He couldn't help but stare at Emily's huge stomach while they chatted with Mitch. Laci would look like that in a few months, and there would be no avoiding the subject or pretending it wasn't real.

At Mitch's signal, Zack brought the snow blower they were there to pick up to the front of the store and was face-to-face with Emily and her protruding stomach. She and Lily stayed in the warm store while Joe and Mitch carried the snow blower out to Joe's truck.

"How's married life, Zack?"

"It gets better every day." Now that he and his wife were kissing on the couch every night and planning out their future together, that was true.

Four-year-old Lily was trying to see what her daddy was doing, and she reached up to Emily.

"I'm sorry, Princess. I can't pick you up right now."

Zack stepped over to her. "Come here, Lily. I'll show you." He picked her up and put her on his shoulders.

She pointed to the box they were securing in the back of the pickup. "It's gonna blow snow in the sky!"

Emily laughed. "She thinks she's going to get to play in the blowing snow. We keep telling her it's not like a sprinkler."

"Mr. Zack, do you have a sled here?"

Emily smiled up at her daughter. "Ahh, yes. The other thing we're here for. Thank you for reminding me, Lily."

"Do I have a sled? Of course I have a sled! I have even more than one." He bounced up and down. "Ready to go see them?"

The little girl clapped her hands and kicked her feet. Not wanting her to fall, Zack reached up to pull her from his shoulders, then carried her like a squealing airplane over to the sled display.

He stood watching while Emily and Lily debated about the different sleds. He couldn't take his eyes off Lily. With her blonde hair and exuberance, she could be Laci's child. All that was missing was the curls. Watching the mother and daughter in front of him, he realized one would never know that they were not bio-logically related and that Emily was technically Lily's stepmother.

Lily pointed at the sled she wanted and looked up at Zack. "That's my Gotcha Day present."

He thought he misheard her and looked to Emily, who was smiling adoringly at her.

"Tomorrow is her Gotcha Day. Tell him what that means, Lily."

"We get to go see a judge and eat cake and ice cream."

Emily chuckled as she turned to explain further. "I'm adopting her tomorrow, so we're celebrating."

"Wow, congratulations!" *See? Adoption is good.*

"Thanks!" Zack thought Emily's face might break from her grin as she looked at her daughter. "I didn't realize how excited I would be. She became my daughter in my heart as soon as I knew Joe and I were going to get married, so it seemed like a formality, but now that I get to be her mother officially, it's like putting a big bow on our family."

"Well that's great for all of you. Come here, Lily. We have some suckers up here that are for special occasions." He walked to the counter and pulled one out of the jar. "Can you save this for tomorrow?"

She reached out her little hand, and Zack studied her face when she took the gift and thanked him. He tried shoving thoughts of what Laci's child would look like from his head.

When Mitch and Joe walked back in, Zack was glad for the change in conversation. He handed the sled to Joe, said his good-byes, and headed quickly back to the office.

Whoa.

Chapter 32

LACI SAT ON THE chair in her bedroom and stared at her phone. The snow storm had given her a good excuse to cancel the appointment with Marianne, and she didn't want to make another one.

She was only fourteen weeks along, so there really was no rush. They couldn't put the appointment off forever, but she wasn't ready to answer questions or choose adoptive parents yet. She wanted to be the baby's mother and wished Zack could be the father. Pulling her blanket from the basket next to her, she set her phone down and pulled the pregnancy book out of its hiding place in the bedside table.

Reading about the baby's development was usually interesting to her, but the timing couldn't have been worse. After trying to focus only on the biology of what was happening inside her body and finding herself unable to cut off from what was happening inside her heart, she closed the book, went to her bed, and let out the sobs that had been building.

She didn't hear Zack come in the front door. He must have heard her, though, because the next thing she knew, he was climbing onto the bed behind her and putting his arms around her. Having him there and feeling his comfort only made the tears gush out faster.

"I don't know how I'm going to be able to do this, Zack."

"Me either."

LACI MUST HAVE CRIED herself to sleep, because she woke up a few hours later with Zack's arms still around her. He had fallen asleep too and was breathing softly behind her. She felt safe and warm and wished time would stand still so she didn't ever have to leave that moment.

When his breathing changed, she knew he was awake and stroked his arm. He tightened his grip on her and kissed her cheek. "Are you feeling better?"

She nodded. "I feel better having you here." She freed herself from his grasp only enough to turn around to face him and put her arms around him. It was the first time they held each other lying down that way, and she wished they could stay like that forever.

He kissed her forehead. "Are you hungry?"

"Yes, but I don't want to move. This feels so good to be here with you like this."

"Yeah, it does. I'll come visit you here and hold you like this anytime you want me to."

"I want you to hold me like this all the time." She propped herself up to look at him. "Thank you for coming in here today. It was a hard day."

"Did something happen?"

She felt the tears coming back. "I couldn't get myself to reschedule the appointment with Marianne."

Instead of chastising her, he looked at her tenderly and covered the hand she had rested on his chest with his. "Do you have to meet with her yet? Why don't you put it off for a while?"

"Do you think that would be okay?"

He pulled her back to him. "You don't always have to please everybody, Laci. This is too big to do it someone else's way, and if you need to take some time before we go back, you should do it."

"Really?" Relief ran through her as she snuggled into his embrace.

"I'll support whatever you want to do."

"I want to wait. I need more time."

"Then that's what you'll get. We've got months to make the decision final."

Chapter 33

A FEW DAYS LATER, Zack and Laci did victory dances in their chairs across the table from each other. It had been a while since they had beaten Mom and Wyatt in Spades, and winning tasted sweet.

Wyatt gathered the cards to shuffle them. "Cynthia, correct me if I'm wrong, but aren't these the same two people who always accuse us of being obnoxious winners?"

Zack and Laci turned and stuck out their tongues at Wyatt.

"I told you they were going to do that. You owe me a dollar." Wyatt held out his hand toward Mom until she dug a dollar bill out of her pocket.

Zack laughed. "These two sure are funny. Laci, when the day comes that you accuse me of being immature, just remember that she raised me and he had a lot of influence."

"Oh sure, blame the mother." Mom shook her head as she got up from the table. "Who needs more cider?"

Everyone raised their hands. "Aye!"

When she returned to refill their glasses, Zack wiggled his eyebrows at her. "Do you have the guts for a rematch?"

She and Wyatt shared a look, then Wyatt spoke. "Actually, we were hoping to talk to you about something. Let's all go into the living room for a family chat."

Zack looked at Laci, and her eyes were wide as they communicated the unspoken question. *Could they know?*

Wyatt and Mom sat in the two chairs, leaving the couch open for Laci and Zack. He was glad to be able to sit next to her if this was going to be an uncomfortable discussion.

Wyatt cleared his throat and leaned forward, looking intently at Zack. "Your mom and I have been having a lot of conversations about the changes coming when we get married in a couple of months. As we've talked and prayed, there's something that has come to mind for me over and over, and it involves you."

"Me?"

He and Mom nodded.

He rubbed his hands together, almost like he was nervous. "Over the years that I've lived across the street, you and your mom became family to me. You were the first one I had the relationship with back when I used to pay you twenty bucks to help me out with things, and you were the reason your mom and I got to know each other."

Zack nodded, waiting for the questions about Laci's baby.

Wyatt cleared his throat again. "You've been the closest thing to a son that I've ever had, and I would like to make that relationship official when your mom and I make ours official."

Zack was thrown for a loop. "I'm not sure what you're saying."

Wyatt exchanged another look with Mom and let out a big breath. "I would like to adopt you."

Zack's shoulders released their tension. "Adopt me? You know I'm an adult, right?"

Wyatt and Mom chuckled. "We didn't know about adult adoption either, but when we went to talk to the attorney about changing our wills and combining our assets, he told us about it. Since your grandparents didn't allow Kirk's name on your birth certificate or allow him to marry your mom, all that's needed is your agreement."

Wow. "Is this because I keep calling you Dad?" He had jokingly called him that several times since Wyatt and Mom started dating, but never thought much about it.

Wyatt laughed, then looked him in the eye. "It's because I want to be your dad." Zack noticed the mist in his eyes for the first time.

"You're serious?" His own eyes stung. He avoided looking at Mom, knowing she would have pools in hers.

"As serious as I am about being your mom's husband."

Zack looked at Laci. She looked as stunned as he felt. She smiled at him through her tears and squeezed his hand.

He stood and extended his hand to Wyatt. "You've been like a dad to me for a long time. I would be honored to be your son."

Wyatt shook his hand and pulled him in for a hug. Mom and Laci joined in, too, then Laci slipped quickly away to the bathroom.

Mom's brow furrowed as she watched her go. "I'm sorry, I didn't even think about how talk of fathers might affect her so close to losing her own."

"I'll go check on her." Zack went and waited by the bathroom door, then pulled Laci into his old room when she walked out. "Are you okay?"

She fell into his embrace and wrapped her arms around his waist. "I am now. The word 'adoption' just hit me. Did they notice?"

"They assume it was because of your dad."

"Good." She squeezed him tightly. "We're not going to talk about me though. I'm so happy for you. You finally have a dad!"

He was still in shock about the whole idea. "It's going to take a while for this to sink in. That's the last thing I expected him to say."

He sat down on the bed and she sat next to him, taking his hand and ready to listen. "Even when Kirk was around, I never felt like I had a dad. I just remember being told to shut up and being scared when he was home. I always had my grandpa, so he was kind of like a grandpa and a dad."

When he and Mom lived with Kirk, there was no fishing or bike riding or throwing a ball in the back yard. There was only an angry, scary man who yelled at him between long-haul trucking jobs—and who told him it was his fault that he had to take that job and couldn't teach school anymore. Zack wouldn't understand until he was much older that it was Kirk's choice to get romantically involved with an underage student that lost him his teaching career. When he left town after Zack and Mom moved out, they never heard from him again.

Laci squeezed his hand. "It almost feels like redemption, you know? You had a bad dad, then you had no dad, and now you get a great dad."

"Yeah, Wyatt has been like a dad for a long time, so it kind of makes sense to make it official."

She pointed at the state championship plaque on Zack's wall. "Remember in high school? He was at more of your football and baseball games than a lot of kids' real dads."

Zack smiled, remembering seeing Wyatt in the stands with Mom, cheering just as wildly as the other fathers there. "Yeah, he really stepped in when Grandma and Grandpa moved to Florida and Mitch went into the Army. That was when he started coaching too."

She smiled. "That's pretty cool. What do you think?"

"That even though I've never heard of a grown man being adopted, I like the idea of it. I'm excited to do it."

"Yay!" She threw her arms around him and gave him a congratulatory kiss. When he didn't let her go, she looked around the room and got that Laci sparkle in her eye. "Not to change the subject or anything, but have you ever kissed a girl in your room before?"

He grinned and pulled her closer. "No, but I probably should before my mom turns it into a girly-looking guest room."

"Yes, you should probably do it now."

The next few minutes were the best he'd ever spent in that room.

Chapter 34

THE NEXT NIGHT LACI was lying in bed trying her hardest to concentrate on the book she was struggling to read. She couldn't believe she was in bed alone on her first Valentine's night as a married woman.

Zack had taken her to a romantic candlelight dinner at the Birchwood Inn and had given her a new wedding ring to replace the one he had so hastily bought when they decided to get married. The dinner was perfect. Their kissing and caressing on the couch had gotten so heated that she was sure they would finally let nature take its course. It had been almost a month since they had decided they were staying married and had moved into the apartment, and their nightly chat and make-out sessions were Laci's favorite activity. Coming into the bedroom alone and leaving him in the living room, on the other hand, was getting harder with each passing day.

Zack was being very careful about not pushing things and always stopped before they went very far. She appreciated his commitment to not pressure her, but she was starting to wonder why he was holding off so much. Despite the signals she had attempted to give to show him that she was ready to take the next step, every night he walked her to the bedroom door, gave her a quick kiss goodnight, then immediately took a shower. A shower that she was certain had only cold water.

She put her book down when she heard him turn off the shower. It was Valentine's Day, and she was taking charge. They were married, after all. They should be able to act like it in every way.

Pulling the negligee set from the box in the closet, she tried it on. It still fit, but barely. She could see under the door that the only light on in the living room was from the TV, so it would be dark enough for her to feel comfortable. After fluffing up her hair, putting on lip gloss, and taking a deep breath of courage, she opened the bedroom door.

In a lightning-fast motion, he grabbed the blanket and pulled it over his lap. When he looked at her, his jaw dropped.

"Wow!" Even in the dark room she was sure she saw him blush. "You shouldn't walk around dressed like that in front of me."

"Or maybe I should." She focused on walking toward him and tried not to lose her nerve.

When she got to him, she sat on his lap. It felt different without the prosthesis she'd grown so accustomed to.

"What are you doing?"

She put her arms around his neck and whispered, "You know what I'm doing." When she kissed him, he responded with even more passion than usual, but stopped.

"Laci, no. You don't have to do this for me."

"I'm doing this for me."

The next kiss was even more enthusiastic, but he pulled back even more abruptly. "I thought we were taking things slow."

She was confused. He kissed her like a man full of desire. She was sure that he wanted her as much as she wanted him.

"Zack, what are we waiting for? We're married and going to stay that way."

"I just don't want to rush you, that's all." He gently pushed her off his lap and reached over for his prosthesis, pulling it under the blanket to put it on and covering himself more fully.

She finally got it. He wasn't holding back for her. It wasn't about not rushing things at all.

Humiliation shot through her like a bullet. He wasn't as interested as she thought or hoped.

Standing on wobbly legs, she walked as quickly as she could to the bedroom without looking back. She managed to hold her tears until she shut the door behind her, but only barely.

THE NEXT MORNING, LACI stayed in her room until she heard Zack leave for class. It was his long day, with an early class and then a shift at the hardware store, so she wouldn't have to face him until after dinner. The texts during the day were few and far between, and she struggled with what to say to him. Neither mentioned what had happened, but it felt like a cloud was hanging over them. When he said that he had to work late, relief hit her before the sadness rolled in.

Crackers and cheese weren't much of a dinner, but she didn't feel like preparing or eating anything more. Thinking about the sting of Zack's rejection and Ronnie's cruel words about her figure, she ate just enough to stop her stomach from growling. She had believed Zack when he told her that she wasn't fat and that he loved her figure, but his actions showed that he was just being nice. He liked her lips, but that was all.

It was ironic, really. Ronnie only wanted her body. Zack wanted everything but that. If she could only have one of the two situations, she would choose what she had with Zack a million times over, but she wanted the whole package for her marriage.

She wished there was someone she could talk to, but she and Zack were the only ones who knew their secret. As far as everyone knew, they were happy newlyweds who were probably going after each other like bunnies. Up until the moment he pushed her away, even she didn't know that the marriage was still a sham.

Zack's Bible caught her eye from its spot on the end table and drew her like a magnet. Hers was still packed away, and it had been months since she had opened it. As much as he encouraged her to end her self-imposed exile from God, she was sure he wouldn't mind if she read it.

She started flipping through the pages, reading the verses he had highlighted. Seeing how many were the same as the ones highlighted in her own Bible comforted her and made her feel close not only to Zack, but to God. The gap that had grown over the past two years as she had gone farther into sin and shame was finally shrinking.

When her eyes fell on 1 John 1:9, they filled with tears. The verse might as well have jumped right off the page and stood on her nose. Being reminded that God not only forgave sins but purified His children when they confessed was exactly what she needed. Her head had always known that truth, but shame over her choices had hidden it from her. Now it was as if God was shining the light on it just for her.

The One who knew their secret, the One who knew everything, had heard her all the times she had confessed her sins. He had already forgiven and purified her.

Purified. He purified me. And He still loves me.

She pictured herself at the foot of the cross. Jesus' blood dripped down onto her, but instead of soiling her, it cleansed her. When it touched her skin, it turned from red to a bright light. Her skin had a glow to it, and her spirit felt light for the first time since she had begun to feel so weighed down by her own choices and mistakes.

It was as if God himself was sitting there with her, holding her in His arms. She was sure that if she opened her eyes, she would see Him there.

Feeling closer to her heavenly Father made her relationship with Zack look different too. Zack showed her in every way but one how much he loved her. He had not only married her in her time of need, but he listened to her and encouraged her and sought out her opinion. They spent hours talking about their future, from having children to throwing around ideas for what kind of business they could start together one day that could work in tandem with the hardware store. They were a team. He took care of her and let her take care of him.

They had their whole lives to continue developing their relationship. Unlike with Ronnie, she didn't need to be someone else or work to get Zack to love her. Knowing that he already did gave her the motivation she needed to do the work to make herself more appealing to him. Maybe someday their marriage would expand into more than an intimate and committed friendship with a lot of kissing, but she would be content with what she had for the time being.

She leaned her head back and basked in her newfound freedom and peace.

Chapter 35

Zack opened the door quietly, not wanting to wake or scare Laci. He had stayed at the hardware store until he was sure she would be asleep.

The store had closed on time, but he had hung around and done some deep cleaning. It gave him reason to stay away from the apartment and would be a nice surprise for Mitch when he arrived the next day.

In truth, Mitch probably wouldn't notice, but it gave Zack something to do. After telling Laci he was working late, he didn't want to turn into a liar. It was bad enough that he was a coward, hiding out from the wife he didn't know how to face.

When he stepped into the apartment, he saw that her door was open but her bed was untouched. He turned his head toward the couch, and there she was, sleeping peacefully and clutching the book she must have fallen asleep reading. After turning down her sheets and comforter, he went to the living room to carry her to bed. When he pulled the blanket off of her, he realized what book she was holding and gasped. *Oh, thank You, Lord.*

The next morning, Zack woke to the sound and smell of bacon and eggs. Knowing he couldn't very well avoid Laci, he tried to act natural.

"Morning."

"Good morning. Did you get everything done yesterday?" Her smile was as bright as the sun.

"I did. Sorry I was out so late."

She carefully basted the eggs with bacon grease. "It's okay."

"That smells delicious."

"Thanks." She smiled at him again. It was as if she had forgotten what a jerk he was the other night.

He knew he had hurt her when he had rebuffed her, but he didn't know how to fix it. It wasn't like he could tell her that he didn't want her to see or feel his leg without the prosthesis on. His panic when she walked into the room had taken him by surprise, and he was still trying to figure it out.

Turning down what she had offered was one of the hardest things he had ever done. When she walked in looking like that, he had felt it in every part of his body. If he hadn't been such a coward—or if he still had two legs—he would have jumped at the chance to finally be with her and would have had the best night of his life. The image of her in the outfit that flowed over her curves in all the right ways had not left his mind since, nor had the wish that it could have ended differently.

She was focused on the stove, but he walked up behind her and put his arms around her and kissed her on the cheek. "I love you, Laci."

He heard the catch in her voice when she said it back to him and leaned into his embrace.

When they sat at the table, she reached out her hand and looked at him expectantly. Usually he had to instigate the mealtime prayers. It was nice to see her back to how she used to be before the cloud came over her and she started hiding from God.

As he was praying for their food and the day ahead, he felt compelled to thank God for their marriage and for giving him the priceless gift that was Laci. Tears misted her eyes when she looked up and smiled at him again.

"You're different today. You look like Laci again."

"I feel like Laci again. I had some good time with God last night." She broke into a grin.

"I saw that. I like coming home after a long day and seeing answers to prayers."

She reached out and put her hand on his arm. "Thank you for keeping the prayers going for me when I couldn't, Zack. You're a good friend."

Friend? I thought I was husband now. He had blown it even worse than he thought. "I'm sorry about the other night. You just took me by surprise."

"It's okay, I understand." She looked down and put the rest of her bacon on his plate. "I'm going to go sign up for the fitness center today after work."

"That will be nice. The hardware store is my fitness center." He smiled at her but saw something in her eyes as she pushed away her half-full plate.

"Are you feeling sick again? I thought the morning sickness was over once you got to the second trimester."

She looked at the plate and shook her head, avoiding his gaze. "I need to watch what I'm eating more."

"I thought you weren't supposed to go on a diet when you're pregnant."

"I know, but I also don't have to eat like a horse."

As she got up from the table and started toward the sink, he realized that she had brought up the fitness center and stopped eating her breakfast after he brought up the other night.

Oh, geez. What did I do? He knew that Ronnie had somehow filled her head with lies about what she looked like, but he had thought he'd convinced her of the truth weeks ago.

"Laci, wait." He stood and walked over to her. "Are you talking about the fitness center and not finishing your breakfast because of the other night?"

She avoided his gaze. "I know men want attractive wives, so I'm going to work on it. For you."

He stopped her from scooting past him and wrapped his arms around her. "I already have an attractive wife—a beautiful one, as a matter of fact." If she knew the way he burned for her every night as he tried to sleep, she would never doubt her attractiveness for one second. Cold showers and forcing his thoughts onto other subjects had nothing on her.

"You're very sweet, but you don't have to say that." She kissed him on the cheek. "It's really okay. I understand."

He reached over and picked up the plate she had just set on the counter and pulled her toward the table with him. "Come on, finish your breakfast. You're supposed to be eating for you plus a baby, not just a baby."

"Zack, it's okay. Really."

He set her plate back down on the table and held her tightly.

"Laci, if you got any idea from me that you need to lose weight, then I'm really sorry. You're perfect just as you are, and you're supposed to be gaining weight when you're pregnant, not losing it."

She didn't say anything but held onto him tightly.

"C'mon, let's finish our breakfast before it gets cold."

Chapter 36

LACI WAS GLAD THE phones were mostly quiet at work and that the items on her to-do list were tedious and didn't require much focus.

She couldn't stop thinking about her conversation with Zack at breakfast. If what he said was true, then she had no idea why he had rejected her.

Now that she wasn't avoiding God and trying to stay out of His way, it was nice to be able to talk to Him about things again. She didn't have many answers, but she felt more peace and didn't feel so alone.

Zack had sent several texts during the day, and they were back to their normal way of chatting back and forth. He said he was picking up a special treat for dinner on his way from class and told her to bring her biggest appetite home with her.

By the time she dropped Roscoe off at Cynthia's and talked with her about some projects Cynthia wanted her help with, she was starving. She hoped Zack wasn't kidding about dinner and meant it when he said she shouldn't diet.

She had just changed into her comfy clothes when she heard Zack walking up the steps. When she opened the door, he had just reached the top step with a big box of Gianni's pizza in one hand and a tub of salted caramel ice cream in the other. *I guess he wasn't kidding.*

"Oh my goodness, I can't remember the last time I had Gianni's!"

He grinned at her. "I haven't had it since before I went to the Veteran's Ranch, so it's been way too long."

"Do I smell an Everything but the Kitchen Sink?" *Uh-oh.* Peppers weren't her friend lately.

"Yes, but I told them to hold the peppers."

"Oh, yay! Thank you!"

They sat together on the couch and watched *The Office* while they scarfed down the pizza and ice cream. He jumped up and put the dishes in the sink, then quickly joined her back on the couch, sitting close to her.

"I want to show you something." He pulled out his phone and pulled up a folder filled with pictures of women.

Great. The competition. "Um, Zack? You know those aren't me, right?"

He gave her a playful nudge. "Funny. Of course I know that. That's the point. What do you notice?"

"I notice that you have a folder in your phone with pictures of girls you've gone out with. I'm not sure I like that."

"That's good, because I don't want you to like it. I just made this folder today to show you something, and I'll delete it when we're done. What else do you notice?"

Just a bunch of women who had your attention at some point. "I'm sorry. I don't have the best brain today. Can you just tell me what I'm supposed to see?"

"Do you see any similarities?"

"They're all blonde and blue-eyed."

He looked at her like an excited kid. "Like you. They all resemble you."

"Okay . . . you have a type." Her brain was starting to hurt and she felt like she was missing something. He was clearly trying to tell her something good, but she didn't get it.

"You are not my type, Laci. My type is you." His eyes danced as he pointed to the phone. "Every girl I've ever gone out with, I've liked because they reminded me of you. I couldn't have the real thing, so I went out with substitutes."

She couldn't take it anymore. "Then why don't you want the real me?" She winced and covered her mouth with her hand, as if the action could take her uncensored words back. After exhausting herself trying to guess all day, she didn't have the energy to stop herself from blurting it out.

"*What?*" His eyes were wide with shock. "Come here." He pulled her onto his lap and slowly ran his hand from her shoulder down to her knee before letting it rest there. "This is my idea of perfect, and I want the real you more than I can even say." He pulled her closer and kissed her tenderly as if to emphasize his point, then rested his forehead on hers. "The other night was about me."

She was even more confused than she had been. "I still don't get it."

He took a deep breath and sighed. "I called Sergeant Richer today and talked to him about it."

"The mentor from the Ranch?"

"Yeah. He helped me out."

"With this?" She motioned between the two of them with her hand.

He took another deep breath. And another. "It was about the leg."

The leg? "Your leg? What about it?"

"I was embarrassed to have you see or touch it."

Oh sweet, sweet Zack. He had let her see the prosthesis when he had shorts on for so long and talked so much about his physical therapy and the phantom pain that he sometimes had that it never occurred to her that it was a problem for him. She put her arms around him and held him tightly. "I'm so sorry. I had no idea."

"He told me that a lot of guys feel self-conscious about it the first time they're with their wives and that I needed to be honest with you."

"Thank you for telling me. I'm sorry that I wasn't thinking of that. I just assumed you were repulsed by me."

"Repulsed?" He let out a laugh. "I'll show you one of these days just how far I am from that. That outfit you were wearing—oh, man." He shuddered as he looked her over. "I definitely want to see you in that again."

The grin on his face convinced her that he meant it, and it emboldened her. This was Zack, her best friend, husband, and the man she had never hesitated with.

"Can I see your leg now?"

He froze and his face went flat. After a split second of regret for pushing him, she realized that he needed her strength. He needed the gentle push from her, just like he had needed it when she had pushed him to try out for the community play with her in eighth grade. It wasn't the same, but it was. One of the best things about their friendship was the way they had always taken turns being strong for the other when they needed it.

She stroked his face and kissed his cheek. "Zack . . . it's going to happen sometime, right? And this is part of us making our marriage real, right?"

"Right, but . . ."

"I know it's not the same, but that's how I felt walking out here in that negligee the other night."

His eyes widened. "You did?"

"I waited until it was dark in here so you wouldn't see . . . you know . . ." She gestured toward her expanding stomach and legs.

"All the stuff I like?" He grinned and pulled her closer and held her silently for a long moment. "Okay, I'll show you mine if you show me yours." He started laughing so hard he almost couldn't get the words out, and she couldn't help but laugh with him.

It felt good to have the tension broken and to have everything out in the open. Her boldness returned, and she didn't have to fake confidence to flirt with him. "You know," she whispered in his ear as she planted kisses there, "the sooner you show me your leg, the sooner you'll see me in the negligee."

He turned his face to meet her lips. The way he kissed her told her she had found the right inspiration for him. He really did want her in every way, just like she wanted him.

There was no turning back now. "I don't want to rush you, but it's not going to fit me much longer."

"Well, then, I guess I'd better get it over with." He sat still for a moment, then took a deep breath and exhaled. She asked God to give him courage and show her how to help him.

"You really want to do this? It doesn't gross you out?"

She shook her head. "It's part of you now, Zack."

"Okay. Let's do this." This time when he gently pushed her off his lap, it didn't feel like rejection. It felt like trust.

"Do you want me to turn the lights off?"

"Please."

When she returned to the couch, her heart was racing and she asked God to help Zack. The prosthesis was propped against the end table and he was doing one of the tapping exercises he'd learned at the Veteran's Ranch that settled his nerves down.

She sat next to him and smiled up at him. "Whenever it feels right to you. It doesn't have to be tonight."

When he looked at her, he looked so vulnerable. Sitting there with her with no prosthesis on had to be monumental for him. He pulled the leg of his sweat pants up and paused, looking at the floor.

She reached over and put her hand on his intact leg. "I love you, Zack. I wish you still had your other leg, but only for you, not for me."

He took her hand and held it for a moment. Taking a deep breath, he carefully guided it and set it on the end of the stump.

She gently ran her fingers along the rough scars. "Can you feel that?"

"Yeah."

"Are you okay with me touching it?"

"Surprisingly, yes."

She pulled his pant leg back over the stump. Moving her hand up to his chest, she passed over many other scars along the way, scars she had seen when the weather was warm enough for him to take his shirt off. She prayed for the scars on the inside as she wound her hands around his neck and pulled his face near. "I love every bit of you, Zack Huntley."

"And I love every bit of you, Laci Huntley. You made that okay." He held her as if he would never let her go.

When he met her lips with his again, there was something different, something even more tender and intimate than any of their other kisses. Sharing their fears and insecurities and treating them as carefully as fragile little shells took her love for him to a new depth. Even though they were fully clothed, in a way it felt like they were 'naked and unashamed' like she imagined Adam and Eve felt in the garden of Eden. Their marriage was as real as any other.

They sat quietly and held each other for several minutes. She got lost in thought, thinking about the women in the pictures. He really went out with them because they reminded him of her? He really wanted her? She meant it when she told him that she loved him, stump, scars, and all. It had no effect on her desire for him. Maybe he meant it when he told her how much he loved and wanted her. He said he wanted her even with a baby belly. They had always made a great team, and this night, this moment, proved it.

Zack finally leaned over and whispered in her ear, "Any chance I can see that negligee again tonight?"

Yes!

She cupped his cheeks and kissed him, making her answer clear. "Give me five minutes and meet me in there."

Chapter 37

ZACK HAD A SPRING in his step as he walked up the stairs to their little apartment after work. The spring had been his constant companion since he and Laci had been enjoying their real honeymoon over the past couple of weeks.

It wasn't just the physical relationship. It was everything. He hadn't realized either the depth of her insecurities or his own until they'd had their "speed bump" as they had come to call it.

He finally told her about how hard he worked to adapt to the prosthesis in hopes that the mental wounds would be healed by the physical progress and how weak he had felt when he was diagnosed with PTSD. She finally told him about the shame she had felt when she admitted to herself that the relationship she was in was actually abusive and the fear of having anyone—and especially Zack—find out.

It was another snowy day and the hardware store was slow, so after he did some cleaning and rearranging, he had started scouring travel sites for a special place to take Laci for a long weekend while he was on Spring Break from school. Since they had spent their official honeymoon doing platonic activities instead of enjoying all the benefits of matrimony, he wanted to do something romantic for her while she was still able to travel.

There were some affordable flights to Florida, so he worked out a way to splurge a little without hurting their plan to save for a house.

When he walked into the apartment, he was greeted by the smell of something burning. He pulled what was left of a chicken out of the oven and opened the windows, then went to see if she was okay.

She jumped off the bed and wiped her eyes when he opened the bedroom door. "I didn't hear you come in—oh no, what's that smell?" She started toward the kitchen.

"It seems to be what's left of dinner." He caught her and stopped her. "It's okay, I took it out of the oven. What happened?"

She avoided his gaze and wiggled out of his arms to get to the stove. "Oh no!" She picked up the chef's knife and started hacking away at the chicken. "I'm sorry, Zack. I can fix it."

He followed her and put his hands on her shoulders. "It's fine. It's just burned on the top."

Her shoulders slumped and she stood staring at the chicken, sniffling. "I'm sorry. I wanted to make a nice dinner for you."

"Blackened chicken is my favorite." Kissing her on the cheek, he tried to lighten the mood. "Oh look, salad! It's perfect."

She didn't respond and focused on cutting the burned pieces off the bird. Even in the height of her hormonal emotional outbursts, she hadn't cried over a little mistake on a meal or been unable to shrug it off.

"Laci, can you stop for a minute?" He took the knife from her hand and set it down, then led her over to the couch.

"I just need to—"

"Stop." He sat and pulled her to the seat next to him. "What happened? You look like you've been crying for an hour."

"It's nothing. I just had a bad day."

He stroked her hand. "This is me you're talking to. What's going on?"

She slumped back against the couch and closed her eyes. "I felt the baby move."

When the tears started again, he knew better than to say anything. He leaned back and took her into his arms.

It killed him how hard it all was on her. She was one of the most loving people he knew, and he had seen her with babies and children for years, even going with her to babysit on occasion. She was a natural and had talked about having her own kids since she was one herself. Every reminder that she wouldn't be raising her own child had to cut right to the center of her heart. He wished they could fast-forward to the day when they could have a child. Or that they could talk about the possibility of raising the one she was carrying together.

He had tried to help her when she seemed sad about the baby, but she usually avoided the subject. When he tried to bring up the idea of parenting, she shut it down. He didn't know what the right answer was for her and for the baby, but he knew he was not succeeding at his mission. He could keep the baby safe from Ronnie, but he couldn't protect Laci from her heartbreak.

"How about if I finish dinner and you stay here and relax?"

"Okay." She pulled the blanket off the back of the couch and wrapped it around herself. "Thanks, Zack."

After he put the food on the table, they ate in silence, she in her own thoughts and he not wanting to say the wrong thing.

She went to bed early, but he was feeling wound up and tried to watch TV for a while. When he finally got tired enough, he joined her.

Sleep came quickly, but so did the dreams. At first, they were about Laci and the baby. He could hear the baby crying, but couldn't get to it. The closer he got to the crying sound, the more it changed.

Soon it wasn't the cry of a baby. It was the cry of a soldier.

Chapter 38

LACI WAS ROUSED FROM sleep by the bed shaking. Zack was moaning, then shouting. She couldn't make out the words but heard the terror in his voice.

She put her pillow between her belly and him so that she could try to calm him down without letting the baby get hit by his thrashing arms. He had told her to leave the bed to protect the baby if he had a nightmare, but she couldn't leave him that way. If he was reliving the moment he lost both his leg and his good friends, she wasn't going anywhere.

"Zack . . . Zack . . . it's okay. You're safe." It took all of her strength to hold onto him, but she managed. By the time the thrashing slowed down, her muscles were burning. "Honey, I'm here . . . I'm here and you're okay."

His breath was heavy. It was starting to slow down, and she kept talking to him, hoping she could bring him out of the dream and into their safe home and her safe arms. Sweat poured off him, but he seemed to be coming back to her.

She didn't let go. "Listen to my voice . . . you're here with me . . . it's all going to be okay."

His eyes shot open. He looked at her without seeming to see her.

"Zack?"

He blinked a few times and sighed. "Laci." When he put his arms around her, he held her so tightly that she could barely breathe.

"It's okay. It was just a nightmare. I'm here."

He loosened his grip but didn't let her go.

"You're not there anymore. You're here in Michigan, in our home with me. It's going to be okay."

He nodded. "I'm okay." As he woke up fully, he looked more like himself.

"Can I do anything?"

"You just did. But you were supposed to leave the room."

"Oops." She stroked his face. "I'll never leave you when you need me, Zack. I help you, you help me, remember?"

"I remember."

Laci woke early the next morning and quietly started breakfast. Zack had told her before that sometimes when he had nightmares, he felt a hangover effect the next day. She hoped that a strong cup of coffee and a good breakfast might help and set about making his favorite crustless quiche.

"Good morning."

She jumped at his voice but turned into his waiting arms. "Good morning. Are you okay?"

"I'm okay. I guess we both had kind of crummy nights last night, huh?"

"I guess so. When we said 'for better and for worse,' we probably didn't think it would be different things on the same night."

He stroked her back. "I'm sorry I woke you. You were supposed to leave the room if I had a nightmare."

"I guess I'm not that good at obeying when you need me."

"Laci . . ."

"I told you on our wedding night that now that we're roommates you can't stop me from helping you."

It was a relief to see his smile. She thought back to some of the articles she had read online about helping spouses with PTSD. One of the things that had stood out to her was a fear that some men had that their wives would see them as less masculine after witnessing flashbacks or nightmares. She squeezed him and gave him her usual good morning kiss to let him know that was not the case.

"Ahh, Laci, what did I ever do to deserve an angel like you?"

She shrugged. "I'm not sure I can live up to angel status, but I'll always try."

His eyes turned serious. "You know that when I woke up in that hospital room with half of my leg gone, I thought I would never be able to have a wife. I sure never thought I could have you. You are one of God's greatest gifts to me."

"You're the gift, Zack."

Chapter 39

THE NEXT FEW WEEKS went smoothly for Zack and Laci. He had a couple more nightmares, and she got used to feeling like a fish was swimming around in her belly. Instead of trying to deal with everything on their own, they were each getting better at letting the other help.

With everything out in the open between them, they both worked at building each other up. He was doing as much as he could to undo the damage Ronnie had done to her, and he hoped that she had stopped believing the flat-out lies she had somehow become convinced of about both her looks and intelligence.

It was still shocking to him that she could ever believe that she was stupid or unattractive. After all, she did have a college transcript and a mirror to contradict those lies. After hearing Mom talk about the tactics of abusers, he shouldn't have been surprised. Seeing Laci fall into it convinced him more than any statistics his mom could come out with that anyone could fall prey to an abuser if the circumstances were right.

For Laci's part, when Zack finally spoke of the guilt he felt for surviving the explosion that killed two of his friends, she gently reminded him of both the mystery and sovereignty of God. She reminded him that they would never have answers to some things this side of heaven, but that God would bring good out of every painful trial they went through.

Zack was drawn out of his thoughts when he pulled into Mom's driveway for Wyatt's birthday dinner. She had asked him to come over before anyone else so they could have a few minutes to catch up. Laci was going to meet him there after work, and Mitch and Bella would be joining as well. It was an infrequent occurrence to have both Mitch and Zack able to be at a dinner on the same day, but closing the hardware store a couple of hours early on a slow mid-March day wasn't going to break the business.

It was important to both Mitch and Zack to honor Wyatt after the way he had helped Zack last spring and had gotten him to safety before he left for the Veteran's Ranch. Wyatt had sat with Zack, Mitch, and Mom several times, making plans in case the anxiety and depression got the best of Zack. When it happened, he helped Mitch and Mom execute the plan smoothly and they got Zack the help he needed. Even though he hadn't been thinking about hurting himself that day, he learned at the Ranch that that could have changed. Wyatt, Mom, and Mitch may have saved his life that day, and he would never forget it.

"Hi, Mom, it's me!" Not wanting to startle her, he always announced himself when he walked in. She had started keeping the doors locked when Roscoe started going to work with Laci, and he knew she missed having him there as her companion and guard dog when she was there working alone. When she had insisted on Laci taking Roscoe to work with her, she did so at the expense of her own comfort.

"Hi, honey. I'm in here."

When he walked into her workroom, she was under a pile of fabric and a sewing machine, as usual. "I'm glad you were able to come early and alone. I'm working on Laci's dress for my wedding, and I don't want her to see it yet. I lost track of time in here."

"Is that it? It looks beautiful." He reached out and fingered the smooth material. The soft shade of green was one of his favorites and would look beautiful on her. Anything would, really.

Mom grinned. "You're picturing her in it, aren't you?"

He hadn't noticed the smile that had formed on his lips. "Yep. She'll look amazing."

"I'm pretty sure that's what she was hoping you would think when she picked that color."

As she carefully folded the fabric and hung it on a hanger, he realized that there might be a problem with the dress. He used the excuse of thirst to go into the kitchen and get his bearings. Mom knew Laci's measurements pre-pregnancy, but since she didn't know about the pregnancy, the dress would probably not fit. He and Laci were going to have to come up with a plan to work around that.

"You and Laci really seem to have hit your stride. I'm happy for you." He jumped when she showed up behind him. "It seems that having your own space agrees with you."

That and a few other things. "Yeah, we love the apartment."

"Remember what Wyatt said about using his house when we get married. If you're interested, you can move in there in a few weeks."

He smiled at her, hiding his real reaction to the reminder. "We're still thinking about that. Is it okay if we get back to you with an answer?" He and Laci had already come to the sad conclusion that the answer had to be no. The pregnancy was getting harder to hide, and they were going to need to spend less time around family. Living across the street from Mom and Wyatt was not going to help them keep their secret. They just hadn't come up with an excuse to give them, and they both hated turning down such an otherwise-perfect offer. Maybe if Wyatt hadn't sold the house by the time Laci had the baby, they could move in after.

"Of course."

Mom paused, looking at the clock. "So . . . I asked you to come early, hoping we could talk privately for a minute." Her strained tone didn't sound like the catch-up chit chat he thought he was there for.

He tried to keep the concern out of his voice. "What's up?"

He followed her back into her workroom and watched her clean up the evidence of her busy day. She avoided looking at him as she dug through the pile of drawings next to her sewing machine, which made him nervous about what she was going to say.

"I don't know how to bring this up without sounding like I'm butting into your business, but I want you to let Laci know that I've been redesigning her dress a little bit." She handed him a drawing of the dress she had just been working on. "This is a copy of my sketch with the new empire waist and wrap. Will you give it to her after you get home tonight?"

"Um, sure." He wasn't sure why she was acting so nervous or why she didn't tell Laci directly, but he went along with it. He looked at the sketch. "Is empire the high-waist thing?"

"Yes. I just don't want her to worry that the dress isn't going to fit." She cleared her throat. "Or cover things."

The look on her face told him she knew their secret—one of them, at least.

"Oh." He kicked himself for not hiding things better. "Mom, I—"

She held up her hand. "You don't have to say anything, Zachary. For whatever reason, you're keeping things private, and I'm trying to respect that. I just don't want her to worry. I know how to accentuate things and how to hide them. Her belly will be suc- cessfully camouflaged, and no one will be the wiser."

"How did you know?"

Her smile was kind even as she contained a teasing smirk. "Well, for starters, I have personal experience in altering clothing to hide a pregnancy, if you'll recall. I also make it a point to be an expert on women's bodies, especially the ones I'm designing dresses for. They are my canvas, if you will." She waved her hand in the air like a snooty artist. She was obviously trying to act like it wasn't a big deal that they had kept it from her.

"I'm sorry we didn't tell you."

"Zachary, your marriage is supposed to be your priority, and the two of you are supposed to have secrets you only share with each other." Her understanding made him feel like more of a jerk.

"Thanks, Mom."

She put down the fabric she had been clutching and threw her arms around him. "Congratulations, son. You're going to make a wonderful father."

Father.

He felt like he'd been hit by another IED.

Of course she assumed the baby was theirs and they were going to raise it. *She thinks she's going to be a grandma.*

He felt sick. The deception that was only supposed to fool the court was going to rip his mother's heart out. What was he supposed to say? He was duty-bound to keep Laci's secret and would not let her down no matter the cost. He didn't respond, but returned the hug.

"I'm sorry you felt like you had to keep it a secret. Did you think we would judge you?"

"Judge us?"

"Son, like I said, I'm an expert at women's bodies—that includes pregnant bodies. I know this baby preceded your marriage."

Shock and the overwhelming desire to protect Laci and the baby silenced him as he stepped back from her. He stared at the floor and gathered courage to do something he never did. Lie to his mother's face.

"Yeah."

"It's okay, honey. The last thing I want to do is make you feel bad."

"Zack, stop!"

His head snapped toward the doorway where Laci stood, her eyes full of tears. "Just stop!"

Chapter 40

ZACK LOOKED AS IF he had just been caught with the crown jewels in his pocket, and Laci felt as if she had demanded he steal them. She was not going to make him lie more than he already had. Not to Cynthia.

She stepped forward to face her mother-in-law. "I'm sorry, Cynthia. We never wanted you to know about this, but I'm not going to let Zack lie to you for me anymore."

"Never wanted me to know?" Cynthia looked back and forth between them, confused. "Why would we not know—" Suddenly her face flashed recognition and fell. "Oh, honey." She reached out and pulled Laci into a tight embrace.

The tears came up from the depths of Laci's soul. Cynthia had always been so kind to her, especially after she lost her mother at the tender age of eleven. She had been a friend, a mentor, and a mother-figure to her over the years, and now Laci and Zack were hurting her. Laci didn't deserve the kindness Cynthia was giving.

"I'm sorry, Cynthia. We were never going to tell anyone. We're working with an adoption agency to find a family for the baby."

Zack put his arms around both Laci and Cynthia as the two women cried.

Cynthia brushed the hair back from Laci's face. "Are you sure? Do you have to?" She was asking mother to mother, and Laci couldn't stop the flood of emotions.

Her knees felt weak. The nearest chair was a couple of feet away, so she started to sit on the floor. Zack reached over and pulled her up, supporting her and guiding her to the living room, where he sat next to her on the couch. Roscoe took his usual post on her other side.

Cynthia sat across from them and quietly handed a box of tissues to Laci. "I'm sorry, I didn't mean to pry."

"It's okay, Mom." Zack kept his arm firmly around Laci, infusing her with strength.

Laci looked at him and back to Cynthia. She hated keeping any of it from her but didn't have it in her to tell the story. "Go ahead, Zack. Tell her everything."

"Okay." He took a deep breath and looked at Cynthia. "Laci found out she was pregnant after she broke up with Ronnie. When she told him, he smacked her around and told her she'd better get an abortion or he was going to do something to the baby."

Having his hand resting on her back calmed her as she tried not to remember that day. She was glad he was the one telling the story.

"We decided to get married so that she could give—release is what they call it—the baby for adoption to a good family. Since we're married, I'm legally the baby's father. I can sign the papers and they don't have to know there's another father."

The shame she had felt from the beginning was only magnified by the compassion on Cynthia's face.

Zack rubbed her back as he continued. "We hate lying, but we're not going to risk the baby's or Laci's safety. If we can help it, Ronnie will never know. God only knows what he would do to her."

Cynthia nodded. She knew better than most women how violent men could be. "I understand. If I can do anything to help you, I will."

"Thanks, Mom." He sighed. "He even accused her of cheating on him with me and getting pregnant by me."

If only. If the baby was Zack's, we could raise her together and be a family.

Cynthia nudged Roscoe off the couch so she could sit on the other side of Laci. "I'm so sorry you're having to go through this." She put her arm around her and kissed her on the cheek. Laci's tears were drying, and she felt some of the weight leave her shoulders. She hadn't realized what a heavy burden lying was.

Suddenly Cynthia's head snapped up. "Wait, is this the only reason you're married?"

Zack squeezed Laci and grinned at her. "Not anymore."

"Oh, thank God!"

Laci finally had reason to smile. "Yes, we're all the way married now. It took a surprise pregnancy and a sham marriage for us to finally admit we'd always been in love with each other, but we're fully together now." *And someday we'll have a baby of our own.*

Cynthia smiled for the first time since Laci had walked through the door. "Well, at least there's that. I always wondered why the two of you never got together."

Zack's laugh filled the room, breaking the tension. "Isn't that a little like the pot calling the kettle black? At least we knew we were in love with each other, unlike you and Wyatt."

Cynthia reached behind Laci to playfully nudge Zack. "Hey, we finally realized it, and now we're going to be married soon. Speaking of that, Laci, the reason this whole conversation started was because I told Zack that I re-designed your dress for my wedding to better hide your belly. But you don't have to stand up with us. You can officially be my matron of honor, but we don't need to have attendants standing."

Laci was touched by the kind offer. "I may have to take you up on that, depending on how well you hid this." She rubbed her belly, hoping the baby didn't understand their conversation.

"Would you like to try the dress on and see? I was going to surprise you with it when it was completely finished, but I would rather have you try it on to make sure you feel comfortable in it."

The soft silk dress was stunning, as were all of Cynthia's creations. The empire waist and flowing fabric hid the growing bump in Laci's middle well.

"I'm sorry that you're having to deal with this, Laci. Selfishly, I'm glad that something happened to make you my daughter-in-law and Zachary's wife, but I'm sorry it had to be this."

"This has been the hardest thing I've ever gone through." She stroked her belly, feeling the baby move around. "But since I can't change the past and make Zack the baby's biological father, I actually wouldn't change any of it. It's because of her that Zack and I are married, and it's because we're married that we finally confessed our feelings for each other. She's the reason I'm married to the right man." She laughed at her weird love story.

"Well, I'm here for you. If I can do anything to make this easier for you, just let me know." She hugged Laci tightly, a motherly, sweet hug. "I love you, daughter."

"I love you, too, Mom."

Laci heard voices in the living room and guessed that the rest of the guests were there. "I suppose we'd better get out there."

Cynthia unzipped Laci's dress and helped her pull it over her head. "Take your time, honey."

Before walking out the door, Cynthia turned and pressed her lips together, simulating a zipper with her fingers.

Alone in the room, Laci carefully put the dress back on the hanger. She prayed as she got dressed, and by the time she had her oversized sweater and leggings back on, she felt ready to go face Zack's—*her*—family.

Chapter 41

ZACK LAUGHED AS HE bent over the small bundle on the floor. As he held his hand up, the baby kicked it over and over, giggling and looking at him with blue eyes the color of Laci's. His hand wasn't tired as he held it in midair, but his cheeks were from smiling so much.

He started waking from the dream and realized that while the baby was indeed kicking his hand, it was still nestled inside Laci's body. He remained still, not wanting their game to stop as Laci slept in his arms. When she started to stir, the baby seemed to wake up more, or maybe it was vice versa.

It would be time to get ready for church soon, but he wanted to stay in that spot as long as possible, holding Laci and Little Bubbles, as he had come to call the baby.

They had sat down with Garrett and Brianna last night and told them about the baby and their plans. Their reaction was the same as Mom's had been, and they offered prayers, support, and whatever kind of practical help they could give.

They had explained it all to Wyatt as well, and once they told Mitch and Bella at lunch after church, the short list of people they absolutely refused to deceive any longer would know. Having the support and prayers of the people who loved them most in the world would make it all bearable. He hoped so, at least.

When Laci started stroking his hand, he knew she was awake. He kissed her on the back of her shoulder. "Morning."

Kick. Zack chuckled. "Good morning to you too, L.B."

They both stayed in place, stroking her belly and feeling the kicks, and he wondered what it was like for her. She rarely said anything about the baby and had talked even less about it over the past few days.

"It's up to you if we go to church. We don't have to if you don't want to."

She shook her head. "No, I want to go."

"Do you remember that Joe and Emily are having the baby dedicated today?"

"It will be okay. We'll celebrate little Sophia." The catch in her voice was matched by her tone of determination.

Two days later, Zack woke up from the same dream. Lying there holding his wife and getting kicked by what with each passing day felt more like their child, he prayed.

He prayed for the baby's health and future, parents and siblings, future spouse and children. God's peace surrounded him even as sadness threatened to engulf him.

He prayed for Laci's peace and for her healing, not only from the heartbreak about the baby but from all the damage inflicted on her by Ronnie and her father.

He prayed for his own wisdom and leadership as a husband and a father when that day came, then for strength to do what was best for Laci and the baby.

Kick. Laci jumped. Zack held her tightly and kissed her neck.

She turned over, which was taking more effort with each passing day, and hugged him tightly. He could feel her tears on his chest. "Zack . . . Can we have a baby as soon as possible?"

He saw his opportunity and took it. "We can have a baby in July."

She pulled back and stared at him. "Don't joke about that."

"I would never joke about that. We need to talk about parenting, just like Marianne said."

"I can't." She pressed her face back to his chest and he could feel the tears against his skin again.

He hated to see her cry, but they had put off the conversation long enough. She was halfway through her pregnancy, and they needed to consider all of their options. "Why not?"

"I can't even think about it. I can't ask you to raise another man's child."

"There is no other man. Ronnie may have started this pregnancy, but that was where his involvement ended." He sighed and rubbed her back. "If we go ahead with the adoption, the baby will be raised by a man who isn't its biological father . . . This is my child now too."

As she held him tightly, he could feel her soft sobs against his chest and the baby's kicks against his stomach.

"I love you, Laci. I'll do anything for you and Little Bubbles."

Chapter 42

LACI AND CYNTHIA WORKED side-by-side on banners for the church's Easter service. Mice had somehow found their way to the old ones and had feasted on them.

"Cynthia, you're especially calm, considering your wedding is in four days."

"I'm trying not to think about it." She laughed. "Not like that. I can't wait to marry Wyatt, but I'm trying not to think about the fact that I still have to wait a few days. I should have followed in your footsteps and done it in under a week."

"Yeah, we didn't really have time to get nervous or think about anything. If we took more time, though, we might have decided our plan was silly."

Cynthia winked at her. "I'm glad you rushed it then."

"Me too."

"You really seem to have hit your stride. I always thought you would be perfect together."

Laci laughed. "Me too. Did you and my mom really talk about it?"

"Yes, we did." Cynthia grinned. "I can picture her smiling down from Heaven and telling me she told me so. She would be proud of who you and Garrett have both become."

Laci's heart swelled hearing Cynthia's words. She wished she had gotten more time with Mom, then thought again about what she would really be thinking. "I'm not sure she would have been happy about me getting pregnant out of wedlock."

Cynthia paused her machine. "Laci, there is nothing a child can do to separate them from their mother's love. You're learning that now, and that's why you're planning to do something that's the most difficult thing in the world—trust someone else to love your baby as much as you do. Don't forget, I have personal experience with how your mom treated women who got pregnant out of wedlock. She was good to me and never treated me differently for not being married."

"Did you and Zack's father ever talk about getting married?"

"Oh, no." Cynthia shuddered. "My parents forbade it, and I was obedient enough to not go against their orders."

"Do you think it would have made a difference?"

"Yes, I think it would have made a bigger mess. My father's best friend was a judge, and he told my dad not to let me marry Kirk or put his name on Zachary's birth certificate so that I would have all the legal rights."

"Why would that matter if you thought you were raising him together?"

"My parents were wise enough to know—or at least to hope—that we wouldn't be together for long. They wanted to make sure that if he or his family ever tried to fight me for custody or visitation, they would have to go to court. They gambled that he would never do that, and they were right."

"I never thought of that."

"Mr. Thomas—the judge—said that most men in that situation were just as happy to not have responsibility for a child, so most of them didn't fight for custody. Zachary's father never wanted to be a father, anyway. He wanted me around, so he tolerated Zachary."

The idea that anyone wouldn't want their own child made Laci's heart feel heavy. "That's so sad. How does someone not love their own child when they're standing right in front of them?"

"I don't know, but thankfully biology and parental love don't have to go hand in hand. Look at Emily and Lily. And Wyatt and Zachary, for that matter. You'll see it when you meet the adoptive parents too. I know plenty of people with both biological and adopted kids, and I don't see any difference in the way they love them."

"That's good." She knew people with adopted kids, too, and knew that to be true. She rubbed her belly, as if to tell the baby that she would be well-loved and very much wanted by her parents.

"Hey, do you want to try your dress on again? Let's see how it looks and see if we need to make any other nips or tucks."

"Okay." She smiled at Cynthia. "Good time to change the subject."

"That's what I thought."

When Laci arrived back at the apartment, Zack was moving quickly around the kitchen. There were two pans on the stove, one with pasta and one with spaghetti sauce, and he had just closed the oven door on what smelled like garlic bread.

"It smells delicious in here!"

"Thanks. I've mastered opening the jar of sauce and heating it without burning it. Did you finish the banners?"

"Yup, all done. They look almost exactly like the old ones, so I think Pastor Ray will be pretty happy." She waited until he didn't have anything hot in his hands to give him a hug and kiss. "I tried my dress on too. Your mother is a miracle worker."

"Yeah?"

"Between the changes she made to the dress and the wrap she made to go with it, this little one is well-hidden."

"Does that mean we're still standing up with them?"

"I think so."

After they finished the spaghetti and gorged themselves on garlic bread, Laci pushed herself to start the conversation she had been too afraid to have.

"I think I'm ready to talk about parenting now."

Chapter 43

ZACK ALMOST DROPPED THE bowl he was carrying to the sink. "Are you sure? Did you talk to Marianne or something?"

"No, I just know we need to talk about it, and I think I'm ready."

He shot up a quick prayer for help. This was his family, and he wanted to fight for it. He just needed to make sure that he didn't try to get his way over what Laci wanted. She'd had enough of that.

"Let's go sit on the couch. The dishes can wait a few minutes." He led her over and sat next to her.

She was quiet for a few minutes. "I'm not really sure where to start with this."

"How about if we ask God to help us?"

"Perfect."

They prayed together, asking God for His wisdom and asking Him to reveal His will for the baby to them, then Zack took a deep breath. "Do you want me to start?"

"Okay."

"When I asked you what you wanted before, you said you wanted the baby to be mine. I want that too."

Tears sprang to her eyes. "You really do?"

"I really do. I love this baby, Laci. I dream about him at night and think about him during the day."

"It's a big thing."

He nodded. "Can I ask you a question?"

"Of course."

"What is your biggest fear?"

She looked thoughtful as she took a deep breath. "It's always been Ronnie. For the past two years, my decisions have all been made because of fear of Ronnie—fear of losing him and fear of disappointing him at first, then after his temper got worse, fear of making him mad. I was so afraid that he would try to do something to the baby that I thought I had to keep her far away from him to keep her safe."

"Ronnie is a scumbag, but I don't think he would do anything to a kid, do you?"

"No." She stroked her belly. "Your mom said something today that made me think he might not be a problem. I was afraid that he would try to beat the baby out of me before because he didn't want to be a father. But men who don't want to be fathers usually just leave, right?"

"It's what mine did." He reached over and rubbed her stomach along with her.

She took a gulp of air and looked at him with eyes that begged for reassurance. "Do you really think you can do this?"

He stopped rubbing her belly and took her hand. "I've never thought about this baby as anyone's child but yours. And frankly, I'm the one who's stepping up to be the father and do what's best for the baby and for you, so I think of him as mine already. I don't want to lose him, and I know you don't either."

Her eyes filled with tears as she shook her head. "I don't want to lose her."

"It's settled then. We're keeping the baby."

Her tears fell over her grin. "We're keeping the baby."

Zack's tears streamed down his face as he carefully leaned over and lifted her sweater up, then kissed her belly. "Hi, Little Bubbles. It's me, Daddy."

Chapter 44

LACI WAS EXHAUSTED BY the time she dropped Roscoe off at Cynthia's house and drove in the direction of the Bay Shore Diner.

After spending the day bobbing between feeling giddy with excitement about keeping the baby and feeling guilty about keeping it from Ronnie, she barely had the energy left to eat dinner, let alone make it. Zack wasn't there when she arrived, so she made her way to the corner booth to wait for him.

When she got settled into the booth, she looked around the restaurant. Her eyes fell on Ronnie, who seemed to be staring at her belly before he met her gaze.

She hadn't noticed him when she walked in, but he was sitting with a woman who was probably his new girlfriend. Laci and Ronnie hadn't seen each other since the day he harassed her at her office, and she felt tension rise up in her chest. It was a small town and she had known that she would run into him at some point, but she wasn't ready. She prayed that Zack would hurry up and get there.

She picked up the menu that she had memorized years ago, wanting to hide from him. *Lord, what do I do?* She reminded herself of the verse Zack had taped to the bedroom mirror that said that God would never leave or forsake His children. She repeated it in her mind while she did one of the breathing exercises Zack taught her from her place of safety behind the menu.

When Zack walked through the door, she exhaled in relief. He didn't notice Ronnie either as he made his way to her.

He leaned over and kissed her before sitting down. "I missed you two today."

"We missed you too." She kept her hand under the table as she stroked her stomach. When they had decided last night that they were going to keep the baby, they agreed to wait until after Cynthia and Wyatt's wedding to announce the pregnancy publicly. They would tell the family tomorrow, but wanted to keep their secret for the moment and celebrate together.

Zack looked nervous, like he wanted to talk about something. After they gave their orders, he fidgeted with his napkin. "I've been thinking about part of our conversation last night."

"Which part?"

He lowered his voice. "The part about men who don't want to be fathers leaving instead of causing trouble."

"Me too. I don't feel right keeping the secret from Ronnie if we're going to be raising the baby in this town."

He exhaled slowly. "I'm glad to hear you say that. I don't either."

"I know this isn't the time or place, but he's sitting over there and I swear he was staring at my stomach when I first sat down."

Zack stiffened. "Did he say anything or—"

Laci put up her hand. "No, we just accidentally looked at each other for a second. He didn't say or do anything, but I saw him looking at my stomach out of the corner of my eye. I think he knows."

Chapter 45

ZACK HELD HIS BREATH for a moment as he tried to figure out what to do. He didn't want to risk a scene but wanted to get it over with.

He laced his fingers with Laci's under the table. "What do you think about me talking to him alone? I don't want to take the chance of him taking it out on you or Little Bubbles if he gets mad."

She shook her head and her brow knitted. "Zack, I appreciate the offer, but I'm the one who got into this mess."

"Did you just call our baby a mess?"

She caught the twinkle in his eye and squeezed his hand. "LB is not a mess, but I don't want you to have to fight my battles for me."

"There won't be a battle if I can help it. I promised you no unnecessary violence, remember? And your battles are my battles, right?"

Laci looked past Zack's shoulder. "His date just left." She inhaled sharply. "He's walking over here."

Zack gave her hand one more squeeze. "Do you want to invite him to sit down and get this over with?" Ronnie might be less likely to make a scene in a public place.

Her eyes were wide as she nodded.

Zack turned just as Ronnie approached their table with his hands up in a surrender position. "I'm not here for a fight." He did seem to be sneaking glances at Laci's protruding belly despite her crossing her arms to cover it.

Zack scooted closer to Laci to make room for their visitor and gestured toward the seat next to him. "Have a seat, Ronnie. We would like to talk to you too."

He tipped his chin in the direction of Laci's belly. "Is that what I think it is?"

Laci nodded, but otherwise remained motionless. She looked terrified, with her wide eyes and frozen face.

"Is it mine?"

Laci stuck out her jaw, showing a strength that made Zack's heart leap. "You know it is, Ronnie."

Zack stroked her hand under the table and looked Ronnie in the eye. "But not if you don't want it to be."

Ronnie exhaled as he looked at Zack, then Laci. "I told you I didn't want a kid."

"Yes, you did. And Zack does." Her fingernails dug into his hand again.

Zack nodded in agreement and worked to keep his tone calm and civil. He could keep his anger in line for his wife and baby. "I want to raise her as mine."

Ronnie rubbed his neck and seemed to be contemplating. He looked directly at Zack. "What's the catch?"

"There is no catch. We just want to raise the baby in peace."

He sneered. "Sounds a little too good to be true." He turned his stare to Laci. "What's your angle?"

"We don't have an angle, Ronnie. We're not like—" She bit her lip and stopped mid-sentence. "We just want to raise our family. We won't ever ask for anything from you."

"Can I get that in writing?"

"If you want it." Zack leaned forward and extended his hand. "You let us live our lives and we'll let you live yours."

"No bills are gonna come to my house?"

What a pig. Zack held his gaze and focused on keeping his personal feelings about the jerk to himself. "No bills. No nothing. Because we're married, I'm legally the baby's father already. All the bills and responsibilities are on us. Do we have an agreement?"

"We have an agreement." When he reached out and shook Zack's hand, it took everything in him not to flinch or vomit. *For Laci and LB.*

Laci looked stunned, and her eyes misted. "Thank you, Ronnie."

"You can thank me with something in writing." He looked away as he slid out of the seat and walked quickly out of the restaurant.

Zack turned to hug Laci, who was shaking. She held him tightly. "I can't believe it! Just like that, it's over?"

"It's over, Bubbles. There's nothing in the way of the three of us being a family." He reached under the table and caressed her belly. *Kick.*

"I think she's happy too." Laci wiped her eyes with her napkin. "I noticed that you said 'she' when you were talking to him, by the way. Do you finally agree that she's a she?"

"We'll find out in a few months, but I figured a guy like him would be more agreeable if he thought he was missing out on a daughter instead of a son."

"You're brilliant. You're in charge of negotiations when she's a bratty teenager."

The waitress brought their sandwiches just then, and Zack smiled as he looked down at the plates, then back at her. "Can we get a double order of chili cheese fries here, please? We're celebrating."

Chapter 46

LACI STOOD BACK, TRYING to stay out of Zack's way. "Are you sure you can get that all by yourself?"

"I'm a man, Laci—"

She giggled at his tough guy act. "Blah, blah, blah, you've been in war, I know. Please don't hurt yourself."

"I do this for a living for the moment. Can you get the door for me?"

She held Cynthia's front door as he carried the big box in. They wrapped it in white paper and put a big yellow bow on it, hurrying to get it ready before Cynthia got home.

Wyatt and Cynthia walked in the door together, and their eyes were immediately drawn to the big box in the middle of the living room.

"What in the world is this? A wedding gift?" Cynthia looked at it from all sides.

Zack put his arm around Laci. "It's not really a wedding gift, but it's something we want you to have here. Sort of a gift for the house."

"Can we open it now?"

Wyatt eyed it curiously. "If you don't, I will."

Zack and Laci held each other as Wyatt and Cynthia started pulling away at the wrapping. Laci couldn't stop bouncing up and down in her excitement.

When they pulled the paper down to reveal the contents of the box, Cynthia squealed.

"A crib! We need a crib?"

Zack grinned. "Well, if you want to do any serious babysitting, you're going to need one."

Cynthia squealed again as she looked between Zack and Laci. "We get to keep the baby?"

"We get to keep the baby." Laci couldn't contain herself when she said the words. It was still hard to believe.

Cynthia and Wyatt pulled Zack and Laci into a big family hug. "This calls for a celebration!"

Laci was happy to accept the offer. They had taken Garrett's gift over to him earlier, so their evening was free. His gift was much easier to transport. It was a framed picture of the ultrasound with a caption on it that read, *Go easy on me, Uncle Garrett. I'm your favorite.*

Zack reached into Laci's bag and pulled out a gift with decidedly more manly wrapping than the crib—a crumpled paper bag—and handed it to Wyatt. "This will help you in your first official act as Grandpa."

When Wyatt opened it and saw the screwdriver, he looked at the bigger box. "I suppose I'm putting the crib together?"

Zack slapped him on the back. "I'll help you out for twenty bucks . . . *Dad.*"

Wyatt laughed and pulled Zack into a hug. "I guess you and I are going to figure out how to be dads together, huh?"

"We are. And we're going to figure out how to put baby furniture together." Zack nodded and winked at Laci. "Starting with the crib across the street."

Wyatt's eyes widened. "You're going to take the house?"

Laci pulled the envelope they had just picked up from the realtor's office from her bag and handed it to him. "If you find this offer acceptable."

"It's a deal!"

As Zack and Wyatt shook hands, Laci turned and looked at the house that would soon be hers, the one where she and Zack would raise all the children God chose to give them. Before she knew it, she was drawn into another family hug.

Thank You, Lord. You've given me more than I could have asked or imagined.

Book 10 in the Summit County Series is coming soon! Follow me on my newsletter, Bookbub, or Amazon to be notified when it's ready.
In the meantime, read on for a peek into the first book in the Hearts of Summit Series, where you can see Officer Brody when he's not fighting crime at Wyatt's side!

A Note From the Author

When I was writing the first book in the Summit County Series (Second Chance), I introduced the first Huntley—Mitch. I had already started writing his book, so I knew a little bit about him, including the fact that he had a nephew who was struggling after returning from war. I chose to only mention Zack briefly in those first books, because I wanted to build his story slowly and wanted him to have healing time before he found love. Way back then, I had a sweet best friends-to-love story for him. Easy peasy, right?

Fast forward a year and a half to when I was writing Garrett and Brianna's story (Returning Home) and Laci came to life. Pretty quickly, I realized that she would be a way better fit for Zack than the girl I originally planned and that they could help each other to heal from traumas. After reading Returning Home, almost every single one of my beta readers wanted to know if Zack and Laci were going to be together. Of course everyone wanted to know Laci's secret too! To be honest, I went back and forth about that and there were two strong options. I finally chose the abuse option so that Laci could be part of Cynthia's healing as well.

One of the things that I love about Zack and Laci is that they knew each other well enough to be vulnerable with each other and to challenge each other. They could take turns being strong for each other and shining truth on the lies they both believed. To me, that's a perfect—and incredibly sweet—love.

One of the many gifts to me as I wrote this story was the opportunity to show how difficult it can be for a pregnant woman considering adoption. Adoption can be a wonderful thing, but it's often dismissed as an easy decision for someone experiencing an unplanned pregnancy. Sometimes it's seen as a given with nothing left to discuss, but it's a unique type of loss and a complicated decision. I worked in private adoptions for several years, and every one of those birth mothers (and many of the birth fathers) loved their babies fiercely and made the best decision they could with their child's future, happiness, and stability in mind.

The topics of trauma and abuse are tough to read about, but my aim is always to give hope. I would love to give a huge list of resources, but in this limited space I can only give a few. Local and national domestic violence hotlines are a wonderful resource for women and men who are in abusive relationships. They offer information, a listening ear, and guidance to anyone who calls with questions (including the question of whether or not what they are experiencing is abuse). US residents can reach the National Domestic Violence Hotline at 800-799-7233 or text START to 88788.

For anyone who has experienced trauma, there are many ways to find relief and healing, including from a local trauma-informed therapist. There have been mentions throughout Zack's story of a tapping technique he used, and because there are several evidence-based treatments that incorporate sensory techniques to heal the nervous system (including ART, EFT, and EMDR), I was purposely vague in describing Zack's technique. As a therapist in my non-writing life, it was difficult to stop myself from stepping out of the story to describe at least one of the techniques in detail! There are so many techniques that can be done anytime, anywhere to send calming signals to your brain just like Zack did that I encourage anyone who has a history of trauma to seek them out.

For those who are not ready to start with a therapist, a resource I recommend regularly for people seeking relief from physical or emotional pain (including anxiety trauma) is the EFTforChristians.com site. It's run by a retired nurse and she has great information about both the physiological and spiritual foundations for using it. For a completely different approach to recovery, there is a course that addresses the spiritual wounds of trauma called Reboot Recovery (RebootRecovery.com), and they offer courses specific to military and first responders. While it's an incredibly supportive environment, it's a *course*, not a support group. I was one of the leaders of one of those amazing courses for veterans a few years ago, and I saw incredible healing in both the veterans and their spouses. When I dreamed up the fictional Veteran's Ranch, I imagined a place that would incorporate all of these wonderful resources, along with maybe some equine therapy. After all, at a fictional ranch there should be horses!

Zack and Laci will continue to pop into future books, including the next one, the as-yet-untitled book 10 of the Summit County Series. Zack's cousin, Taryn, will be coming home for both Huntley weddings—Cynthia and Wyatt's, Mitch and Bella's—and of course she'll have to be around when Zack and Laci welcome their bundle of joy.

If you're feeling withdrawals from your Summit County friends while you're waiting for book 10, I have great news! Stay for Love, the first book in the Hearts of Summit Series, is available on Amazon. You've met Officer Max Brody in both this book and Wyatt and Cynthia's story, and I think you'll love watching him try to figure out what is going on with the mysterious woman who crashes into town with her cute son in tow. He's got a town to protect, and he's keeping a close eye on her—which has nothing whatsoever to do with his attraction to her!

If you want to be the first to see a sneak peek of new books and hear about sales as well as see pictures from the real place that looks like Summit County, please subscribe to my newsletter by following the instructions for the QR code on the last page of the book! Newsletters aren't for everyone, so if you would just like to be notified of new releases, you can follow me on Amazon or Bookbub and they'll email you.

Thank you for spending your valuable time with my imaginary friends. If you would like to leave a one or two sentence review on Amazon or Bookbub so that other readers can be introduced to this book, I would be so grateful! They are one of the best ways for readers to find new-to-them authors and books. If leaving a review is just too much (I get it ~ they take precious time that could be spent reading!), but you'd like to leave a rating instead, you can do that too! Thanks for reading!

See you in Summit County,

Katherine

Stay for Love

Introducing the Hearts of Summit Series

**Sometimes love comes at the worst times and places.
Or is it part of God's plan?**

Officer Max Brody's last relationship left scars on his body as
well as his heart. After swearing off women, his focus is on work
and helping his
grandfather. But when a mysterious stranger and her precocious
son crash—literally—into his life, he's drawn by more than just
curiosity
about what's behind their mother-son adventure.

Ava Barton was still reeling from the loss of her mother when a
hurricane destroyed her home and business. Her trip to a small
town in Michigan is supposed to be a quick one, and her plan is
simple: arrive, do what she's come for, and leave without anyone
knowing she was there. When a
car accident leaves Ava and her young son stranded and forced
to spend time with the cop who makes them both want to make
Summit County their home, her careful plan starts unraveling.

When love takes Max and Ava by surprise, can he convince her to stay and create a family together? Will she see God's hand in their meeting before it's too late?

Sneak Peek ~ Stay for Love

Chapter 1

Ava Barton twisted her ring as she stared at the notes in front of her. Despite committing every detail to memory, there was something helpful about looking at the words again. The fact that the piece of paper hadn't disintegrated was shocking, considering how many times she had studied every bit of information on it in the last month.

"Mom, look!" Oliver pulled her out of her ruminations when he brought the picture over to where she sat on the bed. "I drew the snow outside."

"Wow, you did a great job!" She pointed to the blob in the center of the page. "Is this going to be a snowman?"

The five-year-old wrinkled his eyebrows together as he looked at his drawing. "It's a snow baseball."

"Oh, of course! Now I see it." Only Oliver would combine snow and baseball. Since receiving a mitt, bat, and ball for his birthday three weeks ago, he could combine just about anything with base-ball. Snow shouldn't have come as a surprise.

He peered over at the paper in front of her. "Are you still looking at that?"

"Yes." She swept his hair away from his forehead. "I'm almost ready."

"When are we going to go for our adventure?" His eyes shone. He had been giddy at the prospect of exploring the unfamiliar landscape beyond the hotel window, especially now that snow had begun falling. No doubt he was also catching on to her stalling tactics. He was more than ready to get out of the room after being there for three days.

"We'll leave in a few minutes. Go potty, then we'll go."

He obediently trotted toward the bathroom. *Such a sweet boy.* He had exercised far too much patience while she made excuses to stay in the hotel. Even a five-year-old could only go to the pool so many times.

She paced the length of the hotel room, hearing her mother in her head telling her she was going to wear out the carpet during her stay. What would her mother think of her reasoning for making this trip if she were alive?

Shoving the thought aside, she put on her shoes. She had a mission to complete, and it was past time to do what she had come to northern Michigan for. The first day they had arrived, she had told herself that they needed rest after the long days of travel. The second, she had told herself she needed to study the document in front of her again before she ventured out into the strange world she had invaded—Jack's world. Today she had no excuses. It was time to leave the room and find him. She didn't spend two days driving from Florida to stare at the walls of a hotel room, and Oliver was getting antsy.

She picked up the precious paper and started toward her purse. It was as if an invisible wall suddenly appeared and stopped her—a wall constructed of solid panic.

I can't just go looking for him. What if I don't find him?
What if I do?

She sighed and slumped back to the bed, pretending to adjust her shoe while trying to get her head on straight. What exactly was she going to do if she found him?

Oliver watched her with questions in his eyes as he fastened the strap on his sneakers. He was definitely onto her.

The text message alert sounded, and she swiped her phone open to see the third message in as many hours from her best friend. Sarita wasn't going to back down, and Ava didn't want to worry her. She held up a finger. "Just one second. I just have to answer Auntie Sarita." As she started to reply, an incoming call popped up on her screen.

She hooked her earpiece onto her ear. "Hi Sarita. I thought you had a busy morning today."

"I did, but that was hours ago. I'm grocery shopping now, then heading home. What time zone are you in again?"

"Same as home. We drove straight north, remember?"

"Then why did you—wait a minute. Don't tell me you haven't left the room yet."

Busted. Ava squeezed her eyes shut. "Okay, I won't."

Sarita groaned. "I knew I should have made you take me with you."

She forced a normal tone to her voice, as much to convince herself as Oliver and Sarita. "We were just about to walk out the door before you called." *Not technically a lie, but . . .*

"I can have a plane ticket in my hand in an hour if you need me." Sarita was not as easily fooled as Ava might have hoped.

She smiled into the phone. "You're a great friend. I'm fine, though."

"Maybe this wasn't the best timing for this trip. You've lost your mom, your home, and your business in the last two months. If it's too much to see him now, it's okay."

Rather than bad timing, all the losses made it a perfect time to make the trip. "It's not too much. The insurance company is paying for us to live in a hotel anyway, so why not do this now?" Until the building that housed both her apartment and her gift shop was restored, there was nothing else she could do. It was the right time for this. She needed it. And someday she would tell Oliver about the real reason for their Michigan adventure.

"We're ready to go. Walk us to the car."

"You've got it, girl."

Her hand shook as she once again gathered her belongings, but having her best friend on the phone and her son staring at her with hopeful eyes helped push her to the exit door.

A bitter wind gust slapped her cheek when they walked out the side entrance of the hotel. "Oof! The wind here is as bad as any tropical storm, but it has snow in it." Oliver held tightly to her hand while he tried to catch snowflakes on his tongue.

Sarita's voice was barely audible over the wind. "Is it beautiful?"

She gazed at the whipping snowflakes. "It's gorgeous. The temperature really dropped today, though. Our Florida blood isn't used to this." When they ran to her car, she narrowly avoided falling on the pavement. Why had she put off getting proper footwear? She should have known better, traveling to Michigan in November, but the events of the last two months had thrown her off. Once in the shelter of the trusty Camry, she turned on the ignition and cranked the heat to the highest spot on the dial before making sure Oliver securely fastened his seat belt.

"Give yourself a pat on the back for getting to the parking lot."

"I know you're kidding, but I do deserve something for that. I felt like there was a force field keeping me in the room earlier."

"Well, there's nothing stopping you now. How far did you say the hotel was from his town?"

"Twenty minutes, give or take a few. At least that's what it looked like on the map." She attached her phone to her dashboard mount and opened the navigation app. "It says Hideaway is . . ."

She froze. "It's only ten miles."

Could she do this?

"Talk to me, Ava. Your voice just totally changed when you said that." Her friend's concern was a comfort in the slowly-warming car.

"I'm okay. I'm just . . . I don't know." *I don't know if I can do this yet.*

"That's why I'm here to help you. You need to take baby steps."

As she warmed her hands by the vent, she wondered if she had taken too big a step by driving all the way to Michigan. After all she had been forced to deal with in the past two months, she was about stepped out. "Okay, baby steps. You're right. Maybe I'll just drive to his town today to see where it is. We both need some warmer clothes."

"Now you're talking! Shopping would give you a destination and something to do. If you feel like going back to the hotel after that, you can do it knowing that you accomplished something big."

That sounded like something she could do. She grinned. "You're brilliant. You should be some sort of life coach or something."

Sarita's throaty chuckle reverberated through the earpiece. "Buy me lunch at Pedro's when you get home if they're back open by then. That will be my fee."

"You're on." Ava looked around the parking lot and noticed people driving slowly. They were nothing like Florida drivers. As she pulled out of the parking spot, the car moved funny. She hoped that didn't mean something was wrong with it after the big trip north.

"Okay, I'm pulling out of the parking lot. Baby stepping like a big girl."

Sarita muffled a laugh. "Baby stepping like a forty-year-old."

"Hey, don't rush me! I've got three weeks before you get to call me that." She didn't need reminding of the big four-o birthday that was coming. There was already enough on her mind.

The clouds were thickening and the snow was getting heavier as she made her way down the two-lane highway. "I need to let you go so I can concentrate on the roads."

"Okay, be careful and call me later."

"I will."

"And Ava? Operation Find Jack is officially underway. You're doing it, girl!"

Wow. She really was doing it. She was actually driving to the town where he lived. *Lord, please show me if this is a mistake. I don't really know what I'm doing here or what I'm going to find. Maybe it will be enough to get a look at his town and call it a day.*

In the meantime, she had some shopping to do. Unless she planned to turn around immediately and return to Florida, she and Oliver needed a few things—starting with gloves, judging by how long it had taken to warm their stiffened fingers.

"Are you warm enough back there?"

"Uh-huh."

A quick glance at Oliver showed a boy riveted by what was happening outside the window.

The snow increased as the navigation app took them over hills and curves and past a large blue lake, toward the town of Hideaway. It was a beautiful scene with the fluffy flakes sticking to the enormous trees that lined the hilly highway.

"Mom, we're in a snow globe!"

"It sure looks like it, doesn't it?" The driving was a little scary, but there was no denying the beauty.

"I love Michigan."

"Look at those big trees." She pointed out the window. "They look like giant Christmas trees, huh?"

"This is so cool! I'm gonna draw the trees and snow when we go back to our room."

Unfortunately, the snow also stuck to the road in front of her, making it hard to see the lines. Dodging retirees with terrible depth perception in greater Miami had taught her well, so she could handle a little bit of snow. How different could it be from the torrential rain she was used to? There weren't many other cars on the road here in the boonies, so at least she didn't have to worry about someone suddenly slamming on the brakes or cutting in front of her.

After driving over several rolling hills, she approached a big white gateway that stretched over the road. It was anchored on the ends with two large white lighthouses and had a beam connecting them with "Welcome to Hideaway" scrawled across it. *Kind of quaint. I like it.*

"Look at those lighthouses, sweetie. You can draw them later too."

"Yeah! I'm gonna make them green, though."

"No surprise there." Oliver's favorite color was green, so most of his pictures had something green, whether it was a tree, grass, or even a dog. "Look at this little town!"

The hill the gateway sat atop was the last one, and the town waited below. Off in the distance lay Lake Michigan. She had wondered what it would look like up close, and from this vantage point with the water stretching to the horizon, it looked more like the ocean than any of the lakes she had been to. The familiarity of the view helped her to feel slightly less out of place in the foreign town.

"Wow, look at that, Ollie."

"Is that the ocean?"

"It looks like it, doesn't it? That's Lake Michigan. Remember we saw it on the map?"

"It's big."

A billboard ahead with a picture of two men stole her attention. She inhaled sharply, her breath captured by the faces of the smiling men on the sign.

It's him.

When she finally tore her gaze from his face, she noticed that the speed limit drastically reduced ahead. Never one to flout a rule, she hit the brake.

The car pulled to the left. She turned the wheel, trying to straighten it out. Instead of following her direction, it kept going. *No, no, no, no!*

"Mommy!"

"Hold on, Ollie!"

She pressed the brake as hard as she could, but the car started spinning.

"Mommy!"

"Please, Lord, help!"

Chapter 2

Max Brody was on his afternoon patrol around Hideaway when movement up ahead caught his eye. A car started fishtailing as it barreled down the big hill.

"Everyone forgets how to drive in the snow." He slowed down when it started spinning. "Lord, help that person get control."

He winced when it slid sideways down the short embankment at the bottom of the hill, barely missing the power line. "Nope."

Thankfully the car didn't flip when it jerked to a halt at the bottom, and it came to a stop in a clearing without hitting anything more than a stray branch or two. There probably wasn't any damage, so there was no need to call any backup or emergency responders. He turned onto the side street and parked near where the car had come to rest.

As he approached the vehicle on foot, he couldn't see the driver. A closer look revealed a woman hanging over the console, rear end in the air. His feet moved into high gear and he yanked the door open.

"Are you okay, ma'am?" She ignored him, instead working to get a crying boy's seat belt unbuckled. Max ran around to the other side of the car and freed the boy, who immediately went into her embrace while she hung between the seats. Slowly the woman raised her head and looked at Max, dazed.

"Everyone okay?" The air bag hadn't deployed, and neither of them looked injured.

She nodded slowly, more focused on making sure the boy was okay than answering his question. She sat back in the driver's seat and pulled him onto her lap, soothing him while he caught his breath. Max walked back around to the driver's side door. Her dark hair matched the boy's, so they were likely mother and son. Why didn't they have winter coats on? It was only twenty-nine degrees, and that was without wind chill. He looked more closely at her eyes and sniffed the air to see if she had been enjoying any afternoon cocktails. That would explain the speedy entrance into town that endangered both of them along with everyone else who might have been on the road.

"What happened?" Her green eyes were clear and she didn't appear to be intoxicated, but she was obviously shaken.

"I was about to ask you the same question." He continued his assessment. Her pupils were the same size and weren't dilated. That was a good sign. "Did you hit your head?"

She shook her head, staring down at the boy. "No, I'm okay. Did you hit your head on anything, sweetie?"

The boy's negative response was barely audible against her chest. Max needed to see his eyes too, but he would give him another minute to settle down.

"You were going pretty fast down that hill."

Her eyes flashed in irritation as she rubbed her son's back. "I was driving the speed limit, officer. Something must be wrong with my car."

He worked to keep a straight face. *Slick pavement and bad driving are what's wrong with your car.* "In conditions like this, the speed limit is ten below the posted speed."

She groaned. "How is anyone supposed to know that?"

"Driver's training. Can I see your license and registration please?"

She reached around the child clinging to her to reach her purse. After handing the documents to him, she leaned against the headrest and sighed. "Am I going to get a ticket for going the wrong legal speed limit?"

"We'll see." He tried to restrain his snicker when he glanced at the ID. "Florida, huh? That explains it."

She lifted her head. "I'm really sorry, officer. I've never had so much as a parking ticket." She looked like she was about to cry. If that was a ploy to get him to send her on her way with a wink and a smile, she was about to find out that those pretty-girl tricks didn't work here in the north.

"Stay here. I'll be right back." He walked toward his car to run her ID and check for any active Amber alerts. She seemed honest, but he didn't make the mistake of believing people were as they seemed anymore. After going down the embankment, she needed a moment to calm her nerves anyway. The way her hands shook when she handed him her ID couldn't have been just from the cold.

Her driving record was as spotless as she had claimed, and there were no alerts that even remotely matched the boy. As he approached her car, he noticed that the front wheel was bent at an angle. When he bent over, he saw she had hit a stump. So much for letting them on their way quickly.

"Do you want the good news or the bad news first?"

The look on her face gave a hitch to his gut. Maybe he shouldn't have made a joke when she was so clearly shaken. He put his hands out, hoping to calm her. "I'm not giving you a ticket, ma'am. You just need to slow down and exercise more care when the roads are slick like this."

Her shoulders visibly relaxed as she let out a sigh. "Thank you."

"Your car, on the other hand, is not so lucky."

"What? How can you tell?"

"If you want to step out of the car, I'll show you."

"Ollie, you sit over here for a minute." She patted the passenger seat. "I just need to look at the car, but you need to stay here where it's warmer. You can watch me through the window, okay?"

"Yes, Mom." The boy moved over without taking his eyes off her.

She followed Max around to the passenger side. Before he had a chance to point out the damage, she groaned and bent forward to examine it more closely.

"Oh no." She stared at the wheel. "I knew I shouldn't have left the hotel room."

"I can have dispatch send a tow truck over here to get you out of this and get your car to a shop." He gestured over his shoulder toward Woody's place. "There's one just down the street."

"I don't suppose there's a way to do a rush job on that." The way her eyes darted around and kept looking behind him made his antenna rise. Why was she so nervous?

"I can't make any guarantees, especially on a day like today, but I'll put in a good word for you." The smile that was meant to put her at ease was met with a frown.

She was starting to shiver, and rubbing her arms didn't seem to be doing much to help. Her thin sweater and jeans were not going to keep her warm with the snow and wind whipping off the lake.

"Ma'am, do you have coats in the car?"

She shook her head. "We were coming into town to buy some warm clothes when this happened."

Her lack of appropriate clothing and jumpiness since she had gotten out of the car made him wish that he had been able to get more information from the check of her driver's license. She acted like a woman with secrets, and he had a town to protect.

His radio had been quiet since he had pulled over to help them, so he had a few minutes to try to gain some more information before he sent them on their way.

"If you'd like, you can wait in the back of my squad car while I call dispatch and fill out the report. I've got a blanket in the trunk that will help keep you warm."

Her eyes widened. "A police report?"

"A crash report is procedure, ma'am. It will give you something to send to your insurance company stating that the accident was caused by road conditions."

"Oh!" The visible relief he saw on her face made him wonder what her story was. Either she was so squeaky clean that she had never been in trouble a moment of her life, or she was hiding something. He wasn't going to have a repeat of what happened when he worked in Flint. If she was hiding something, he was going to find out what it was, and soon.

She stepped back to her car and grabbed her purse and a bigger bag. After looking in the direction of the billboard, she helped the boy out of the car, then took him by the hand and followed Max to his.

Print and ebook available now on Amazon!

Acknowledgments

I'm so thankful to God for the way He shows up in the writing process. I had so many ideas about how this story would go, but He had better ones and showed me how He had planted seeds I didn't know were seeds way back in the first book. For example, you might think that I brilliantly planned to have Joe and Emily's baby due at the time that Zack and Laci were making decisions about their baby, but you would be wrong. You also might think that I made Laci blonde so that when Zack looked at Lily, he saw what a child of Laci's might look like. Wrong again. I couldn't ask for a better co-author than the Author of Life Himself.

Friends and family are always part of my acknowledgments, because even when they don't realize they're doing it, they encourage me in a million ways. Even the incessant teasing about when the next book is finally going to be out touches my heart.

I would love to list every beta reader and typo hunter who was a part of bringing this book to life, both in its original form and this re-edited form. Unfortunately, I have such a huge fear of leaving anyone out of the list that I would rather skip it than risk that. They know who they are, and they (hopefully) know that I treasure each and every one of them. And of course my critique partner and proofreader deserve a special mention too!

Readers and followers have no idea how important they are. You are the reason authors go through everything it takes to publish a book. It is my prayer that everyone who reads my books gets a little personalized message from God out of them. You're amazing.

About the Author

Katherine Karrol is both a fan and an author of sweet Christian romance stories. Because she does not possess the ability or desire to put a good book down and generally reads them in one sitting, she writes books that can be read in the same way.

Her books are meant to entertain, encourage, and possibly inspire the reader to take chances, trust God, and laugh in the midst of this thing we call life. The people she interacts with in her professional world have absolutely no idea that she writes these books, so by reading this, you agree to keep her secret.

If you would like to talk about your favorite character, share who you were picturing as you were reading, or just chat about books and pretty places, you can email her at KatherineKarrol@gmail.com or follow her on the usual social media outlets. She's most active on Facebook, where she has a small reader group and loves to talk about books. The next most likely place to see evidence of her existence is Pinterest, where she has boards for all of her books, memes, and other bookish things. She seems to think that Instagram is a place to look at other posts but usually forgets to make her own. Maybe someday she'll get on the ball with that. Maybe.

Books

Hearts of Summit Series

Stay for Love

Open the camera app on your phone and aim it here to get a link to join my email community!

If the QR code is too confusing, just email me for the link :)

Made in United States
Orlando, FL
14 August 2022

21022650R00125